"NEW, ABSORBING, EERILY CHILLING"

—Ira Levin,
author of *Rosemary's Baby*

"It's for readers who enjoy reading late on moonless nights and getting spooked by banging shutters, meandering statuary, blood on the kitchen floor and a bit of sadomasochistic sex.... I was properly nervous."

—*The New York Times*

"A new and big storytelling talent . . . as fascinating and chilly a Gothic as I have ever read"

—Morris West,
author of *The Navigator*

LITTLE
ANGIE

EMMA CAVE

P A KANGAROO BOOK
PUBLISHED BY POCKET BOOKS NEW YORK

LITTLE ANGIE

POCKET BOOK edition published November, 1977

This POCKET BOOK edition includes every word contained in
the original, higher-priced edition. It is printed from brand-
new plates made from completely reset, clear, easy-to-read type.
POCKET BOOK editions are published by
POCKET BOOKS,
a Simon & Schuster Division of
GULF & WESTERN CORPORATION
1230 Avenue of the Americas,
New York, N.Y. 10020.
Trademarks registered in the United States
and other countries.

ISBN: 0-671-81689-6.
Library of Congress Catalog Card Number: 76-39924.
This POCKET BOOK edition is published by arrangement with
Coward, McCann & Geoghegan, Inc. Copyright, ©, 1977, by
Emma Cave. All rights reserved. This book, or portions there-
of, may not be reproduced by any means without permission
of the original publisher: Coward, McCann & Geoghegan,
200 Madison Avenue, New York, N.Y. 10016.
Printed in the U.S.A.

My thanks to M. and B., for the time,
and to S. and P., for the place.

PART I

END COTTAGE

ONE

There had been a silence in the hall as she let herself into the house, a silence which she immediately felt reluctant to break. She glanced at the letters on the hall table: a couple of dull-looking brown envelopes for her. A white envelope, addressed to Richard, lay ripped open and empty. One of his arrogant habits, she thought, screwing the envelope into a ball and dropping it into the wastebasket under the table. It was then that she heard the noise. It was a curious dragging sound which she couldn't identify. Very quietly and slowly, she moved farther into the house, into the silence which had fallen again. At the end of the hall, the dining-room door was open. She went in. There was chaos on the mahogany table. Three empty champagne bottles—the 1959 Louis Roederer—two smeared glasses, two plates that seemed to have held eggs and bacon. Red stains on one of the plates. A bottle of ketchup next to it. On that plate, several cigarettes had been stubbed out. They were red, too. A picture of Kirsty's heavily lipsticked mouth appeared before her eyes. Quite disgusting, she thought, surveying the table. She would have to tidy up before Mrs. Maynard came in to clean next day. (Just the sort of thing Richard despised in her: "For Christ's sake, if you pay people to do things for you, let them get on with it.") She was moving toward the table when she heard the sound again, the dragging. It was quite clear now where it came from—the basement. It must be Richard. What could he be doing down there? Was he alone now? she wondered, glancing at the two plates on the table. More movements, and then footsteps—a sound of hurry.

"Richard," she called. It didn't come out very loud, but she was impressed by how calm, almost languid, her voice sounded. Positively English, she thought, in the again absolute silence. In that silence she left the dining room and started—carefully, slowly—down the stairs to the basement. Slowly, deliberately, her hand holding firmly to the banister, she turned the bend in the staircase to the big dim kitchen. But the floor! What was all that red? There was so much of it. And what was that great lumpy plastic bag? And that foul-sweet smell in the air? Then she was caught up, battered, felled, in his headlong desperate charge.

Her hands were shaking. She pulled to the side of the road. She was glad she had avoided the motorway, even though the journey took a little longer on this A road. What would Dr. Blaumann say if he could see her now? All his doubts would be reinforced. "I myself"—his deliberate speech was still markedly German, although he had been in England since 1935—"am not wholly convinced that you are ready for this . . . undertaking."

"But I must make a start," she had said. "I must make a move."

"That is precisely what I want you to do, Angela. Provided, of course, that your move is in a forward direction."

"I feel it will be," she had said. But it was true that she became tired easily. She was tired now, which was stupid, as she had left London only an hour and a half before. Getting out of London had been the worst part, following all those arrows and numbers—numbers always made her mind go blank—that seemed to be taking her round in circles. And she had felt as if she were drowning in the roar of the huge lorries whose wheels loomed up over the sides of the Porsche. But she should have felt better once she was out in the flat Essex country. The landscape was peaceful, its tones muted by the intense heat. Though the hedges and ancient trees gave her the closed-in feeling she often got from the English countryside. She could never quite decide whether it was cozy or claustrophobic. She remembered, suddenly, a great wheat field in Ohio, with not a tree or hedge in sight; a flat sea of gold except when a gust of wind started a great smooth wave or a moving cloud cast a giant floating shadow. Driving fast, you would be in and out, in moments, of what seemed like a temporary settlement—gas station, drugstore, a few squat houses. Whereas these English villages were so safe, so permanent. Disaster seemed impossible, surely not even a hurricane could uproot them. And what a ridiculous idea a hurricane in Essex was.

All the same, her hands, on the steering wheel, had begun to feel as if they branched out stiffly from her wrists. It must be because she had slept so badly the night before that she was feeling so tense and spiky. And when she had slept, there had been the dreams, so that it had been almost better to be awake. The redness of the dreams washed over her mind now, like a stain spreading. *Don't try to remember,* she told herself. But the red came up in a wave, and receded, leaving a word behind it.

Blood.

"*Control* yourself," she said aloud. She closed her eyes. She flexed her fingers. She recited four lines from her favorite poem, "Christabel":

> The lovely lady, Christabel,
> Whom her father loves so well,
> What makes her in the wood so late,
> A furlong from the castle gate?

She opened her eyes. She replaced her hands on the steering wheel. She restarted the car. Half an hour later, she was in Suffolk.

A few miles the other side of Haverhill—what a depressing little town!—she became alert for the turning off which followed just after where a B road crossed. She didn't remember the country-side. After all, she had only been here once before, and Jessica, as usual, had been chattering all the time. What did Jessica do, Angie wondered, when she was alone, with no one to talk to? She couldn't imagine Jessica doing nothing, just gazing into space, as she herself had done, in hospital, month after month. Though that hadn't been a very con-structive activity, had it? Wasn't it unfair of her to criticize Jessica's hyperactivity? Jessica had, after all, done so much for her, was her closest—her only?—friend. It was five years now since Jessica had constituted herself Angie's guide and mentor, interpreter of the mysterious English.

There was the B road now. A minute later, she

recognized the little tree-covered island where the
road she was traveling on widened. She waited for
a van to pass, and then drove across the road and
around the island. Suddenly she was out of the
sunshine and in a narrow winding green tunnel.
An English lane. The tall hedges fell away, and on
the left was a pink farmhouse. "Mmm, that pink's
rather dreamy," she had said to Jessica. "It's tradi-
tional in Suffolk," Jessica had answered. Angie was
always surprised by how many odd little bits of
information Jessica possessed about everything,
whereas she herself only knew about books and
wine. But as Jessica had once said to her, rather
sharply, a long time ago, "I sometimes feel, Angie,
that you wander through life in a kind of waking
trance." And that had been long before Angie's
illness.

Now there were little golden spans of wheat
between hedges. How still it was, how absolutely
unmoving the grain stalks—not a ripple. She drove
down another steep little lane and emerged in a
village: Foxdene. "A marvelous church," Jessica
had said, and then added something about "misericord seats." Here, in the country, Angie decided,
she would catch up on things like that, would take
an interest in all those *matters of fact* that tended
to go in at one of her ears and out at the other.
Beyond the church, with its little square golden
tower, was the village green, and beyond that,
over a little humpbacked bridge, was the newly
thatched cottage that Jessica had been so scathing
about. On the lawn in front of it was a shiny
green-painted wheelbarrow, rooted in the ground
and planted with red geraniums. On the other
side of the lawn a ring of green and red plaster
gnomes crouched round a small tree. "The bestial

bourgeoisie!" Jessica had exclaimed. "They shouldn't be allowed into the real country at all. They should be confined to the suburbs by law." Angie had laughed, but though the garden was ridiculous and the gnomes were awful, she couldn't help finding something about it rather touching. Someone's fairytale cottage. To ensure that, he had even brought his own fairies—well, gnomes—with him. But Angie would never have dared to express such a *twee* and *fey* view to Jessica, who always made it clear that she deplored this side of Angie. So it was odd, really, that Jessica should be encouraging her in her present project. Presumably on the grounds that doing anything was better than doing nothing.

She slowed down by a small white signpost with uneven black letters on it: Clave to the left—only a mile and a half now. What a cute little sign, she thought, consciously defying an absolute prohibition on the word "cute." Quite different from the signs on the highways with their boring "clean modern design." Another world. Aloud she murmured, experimentally, "It was then that Angie entered another world." Suddenly she was feeling safe, and sure that she had been right to come. This would be right for her; she knew it. Turning a corner, she swerved a little, more from surprise than necessity, at the sight of a car parked, facing her, on the verge. It was an old Rolls with a small man seated behind the wheel, and it was the first car she'd seen since she turned off the highway. An odd place to park, she thought.

Over on the right, now, were those magnificent closed iron gates on which she had commented to Jessica. "Mmm, very handsome," Jessica had said, glancing sideways with a surprising lack of interest.

Through the gaps in a broken-down hedge, she glimpsed a sagging cottage with rotting thatch. Unusual in this well-kept countryside, she thought. Suddenly she was aware of her tiredness again. But she knew that she was nearly there. The lane sloped gently upward. She passed an ugly red-brick house with a broken gatepost, and Clave was spread out beneath her. The square-towered church was the center of the village. Cottages were above the church (Upper Green) and below it (Lower Green). On the right was a big farmhouse—pink again. Little roads ran in all directions: one to the Upper Green, where the pub was, she had noticed when Jessica drove her round the village; another winding, between the church and the farm, off into the distance; and the one she must take now, turning sharp to the right, along the Lower Green. First there was a square white house, too close to the road and with no trees around it. The grass verge widened suddenly, and set back from the road was a black and white cottage, practically buried in trees and bushes. And now the last cottage in the village. She drove up the track onto the verge, and then through the open gateway, and stopped the car on the grass. For here it was. End Cottage. Her journey's end. "And the princess entered her domain," Angie murmured. "Have you always had these fantasies?" Dr. Blaumann had asked her. "For as long as I can remember," she had answered.

The dark king of a dark country—her father. And her mother, its fading foolish queen. He, so upright, rigid in his dark clothes; and she, more

lacy, more flouncy, more Southern belle than the
advancing years allowed. The memory of her
mother's appearance, her stagy Southern accent,
her verbal mannerisms, her determined helpless-
ness, could still make Angie wince. As she had,
from an early age, noticed her father wince.

A memory of having been held between his
knees. She must have been six or seven. He was
angry with her. She couldn't remember now what
crime she had committed, but she could still feel
his hands grasping her shoulders hard, hear his
hard voice, experience his knees hard on either
side of her body. She had started to cry. "I'm
sorry, Daddy." And suddenly he had smiled, had
lifted her up and seated her in his lap, his arms
around her, his chin resting on the top of her
head. Paradise regained. She was forgiven. She
was safe again. His little Angie.

Little Angie. "A miracle, a fairy's gift," as she
had heard the Irish cook once say. Born when her
mother was thirty-nine and her father forty-four.
After twenty years of marriage, three miscar-
riages, and one son—born dead. "A fairy's gift";
the words appealed to little Angie, wispy and
fragile, blond like her mother. Little Angie ran
and skipped. Laughing shrilly, she peeped from
behind the dark carved furniture bought by her
Italian grandmother.

"She's just the image of what I was as a little
thing," her mother would remark with a touch of
complacency, feeling perhaps that in this one regard she had outdone her husband, her fair delicacy having so astonishingly triumphed over the
weight of his impressive Italian-dark good looks.
But even this triumph was only hinted at, the
words spoken lightly, softened still further by a

quick upward glance at him, sheltered by a quick (and *silly*, Angie would think) batting of her eyelashes. Her mother was terribly afraid of him; that was evident to Angie always. Did she sympathize with her mother? No, she despised her.

Her mother treated Angie as a toy. No, that wasn't quite right. As a decoration, as a stage prop. When visitors came, she used to try to arrange little mother-and-child tableaux. But Angie quickly became aware of this and, whining and protesting, would wriggle out of the pretty poses. She was revolted by the scent her mother wore, which was sweet and heavy.

Her mother tried to dress her in cute clothes, covered with little bows and buttons. Angie liked to dress up, but not in those awful things. She liked to wear the clothes she had found in a box in the attic. They had belonged to her Italian grandmother. They were perfect for her many princess roles: peacocky shawls; finely embroidered silk blouses, faded to the color of clotted cream; a velvet skirt, which Angie wore as a cloak— Cinderella hurrying home from the ball. Shrouded in a shawl, she lay on the floor, hands crossed on her chest, eyes closed, lips pouting—Sleeping Beauty awaiting the reviving kiss. Or she would toss on her own bed—the *real* princess, bruised by the pea beneath the twenty mattresses and the twenty quilts.

Those were her solitary games. Then there were the other ones, the ones she played with her father. She loved to tease him, especially when her mother watched with an air of irritated surprise. Of apprehension, too—as if she were waiting for the skies to fall. Which, as Angie herself was always aware, was a possibility. That was the excitement; to go *so* far, to hover dizzy on the border of *too* far, and then, at the last moment, retreat. And see his frown smooth out, hear his tone soften. Safe again. His little Angie.

Growing up, she walked tightropes toward him, eyes fixed on his face. She spent a great deal of time in his company. Partly by inclination, partly because of his weak heart, he worked at home. In the library. In the mornings he pored over his investments, ringing up his broker and issuing peremptory instructions. In the afternoons he was usually surrounded by book dealers' catalogues. He collected books printed by private presses in England and Italy. When he raised his eyes from what he was doing, he would meet the gaze of Angie, curled up on the window seat with her book.

She saw very little of other children. Her father had a contempt for his country and its customs, and constantly referred to his Scottish and Italian heritage. When she was sixteen, her father had promised he would take her on a trip to Europe. (Just the two of them. Her mother was bored by art and sightseeing.) And when she grew up, Angie would go to the university in Scotland where her grandfather, a crofter's son, had lived each term on a sack of oatmeal and a barrel of salt herring. Honorable poverty, from which he had emerged to emigrate to the States, become an engineer, and found the family fortune here in Cleveland. And to make his romantic marriage to a beautiful young Italian governess. "Your grandfather and grandmother were quite wrapped up in each other," Angie's mother had once told her. "So wrapped up that they didn't seem to have much time for your father." And she had laughed, a small, malicious laugh.

Angie didn't go to school. The best teachers came to the house, or she went to them, driven and fetched by the chauffeur. Her father was determined that she should be well educated. That was one of the tightropes: being little Angie and being clever at the same time. She found a way: she was hopeless at math and science. Her father could be indulgent about that, when she was so talented at English and art. As he said, the feminine subjects.

Always, when she was alone, and at night, there were the fairy stories in her head. Only, as she came into her teens, the focus shifted: to the dark figure who kissed her awake, or put the glass slipper on her foot, or lifted her onto his horse and rode into the forest. Steely, faceless, he caressed, elected, acted; limp, she was kissed, chosen, carried away.

She was fourteen the time she went too far. Did she know that was what she was doing, at the time? Wasn't that, actually, *why* she did it, testing herself, testing him? For she hadn't really wanted to go to the party at all. She was uneasy with her contemporaries, and they, for their part, thought her weird: not going to school, living in that huge old-fashioned house, like a museum in the decaying city center, instead of in the safe, airy suburbs ("suburban" was one of her father's most contemptuous words). And she couldn't talk about the things that they did, wasn't remotely interested in sport, or TV, or popular music.

No, really, the only possible reason for her deciding to go was that her father had forbidden it. "Squalid, moronic teenagers" (how delicately he assassinated the word "teenagers"). "Deafening themselves. Swilling beer, and probably spirits. Necking." (This last was a word he slaughtered with savagery.) "Out of the question, Angie." That was the phrase that had started her off: "Out of the question." What *was* the question? Would she ever be allowed to ask it? And would she ever hear the answer?

When she let herself into the house, she knew he would be waiting. He was standing at the foot of the stairs.

"Well?" he said, after a pause in which coldness, silence, wrapped her round like a fog. "What have you got to say for yourself? As a matter of fact," he continued, "I don't think I'm really interested in hearing it."

"Oh, *Daddy*," she said, taking a step toward him, then stopping, because his immobility was so intimidating. She exerted herself to take another step (*every step the Little Mermaid took was like treading on sharp tools and pointed knives*). She even produced a high little giggle. "You were quite right, Daddy," she said. "The party was awful. I was so bored."

He didn't move a muscle. His coldness seemed to be seeping into her bones. But, like Kay in *The Snow Queen*, she felt there was a splinter of ice in her own heart, too. There was something in her, saying, "I shall not yield." Yet, at the same time, she felt an overwhelming impulse to sink to her knees. Yes, that was it! But of course she could, she would, do no such thing.

"I'm sorry, Daddy," she heard herself saying in a tone that was almost perfunctory.

He just looked at her. "Come," he said. He started to ascend the stairs and she followed him.

He led the way to her room. He opened the door and went in ahead of her, but only to take the key from the lock inside. "I can't trust you any more," he said. She clutched wildly at his arm.

He removed her hand quite impassively. He went out of the room, shutting the door behind him. She heard the key turn in the lock. "Daddy," she called. "Daddy!" His footsteps went away, down the passage. She sat down on the bed and tried to sort out all the things that were going on inside her head; it felt as if they were happening in her chest and stomach as well. She was frightened, yes. And humiliated. Locked in her room like some child in a Victorian storybook. But the splinter of ice seemed to be growing into a stalactite. And beyond this, below it, was a terrible feeling of being cut off—from the source. And, coexisting with all this, was—what? A curious sense of anticlimax. *Because nothing had happened.*

It was eleven next morning when he came in. She had been awake since six, and she was very hungry. She hadn't been able to decide on any course of action. She had thought of banging on the door, but what would have been the use of that? No one would respond without her father's permission. And she couldn't have borne her mother to hear her futile efforts.

"I have decided," he said, "that you are going to stay in here until you promise never to disobey me again."

"But, Daddy," she said, "I told you I was sorry. I am sorry. Truly, I apologize. But how can I make a promise like that? How can I know what's going to happen in the future?"

"All the same, you will stay in this room until

you make that promise. And you can have water"
—he gestured to the door that opened into her
bathroom—"but you can't have food."

"Daddy"—she attempted a tone of plaintive appeal—"I'm so *hungry*."

He ignored that. "When you are ready to promise," he said, "ring the bell. I will tell Jane to come
and open the door, and you can come down to the
library."

Later she would be astonished that she had
stayed in that room for two days. The hunger
helped in a strange way. Ignoring it was something to concentrate on.

The first day was a dull day, but not dreadful.
It was a day in a vacuum.

The second day moved with a different kind of
slowness. She was beginning to feel so weak and
strange. How she longed for her father. He was
what she was missing most of all. But . . . she
couldn't give in. The splinter of ice sent her to
Hans Andersen to read *The Snow Queen*. When
she came to the place where the ice in Kay's heart
was melted with tears, she started to cry herself.
She put the book down.

For most of that night she seemed to be half
awake and yet dreaming. Great horses reared their
hooves in the air, then pounded remorselessly over
hard white sand. It wasn't till early in the morning
that she really fell asleep. When she woke, it was
ten o'clock. Her mouth was dry. Her eyes ached.
She could feel her heart beating. She must give in.
Because she wanted to. She knew that now.

Slowly, luxuriously, she took a bath. She
combed her hair. She dabbed cologne on her
wrists and behind her ears. She put on one of her
favorite dresses, which had a pattern of little

stripes and roses. Then she rang the bell. A minute or two later, eyes popping, Jane came up to open the door. "Good morning, Jane," said Angie, and, head held high, walked past her.

Her father had just been brought the split of champagne which he drank every morning at eleven. The glass was raised to his lips. She watched the little golden bubbles rising to the surface. He sipped judiciously.

He drank in a conscious, measured way, always. He also drank a great deal, she would realize later. Always wine—he never touched spirits or beer. The champagne at eleven; wine at lunch; sherry before dinner; wine with dinner; port, or sometimes Madeira, afterward. Always the best. "Buying good wine is one of the most sensible things one can do with money," he had said to Angie. The amount he drank never seemed to affect his behavior in any way. At the time, it didn't seem to her any more surprising that he should drink so much wine than that she herself should down pitchers of homemade lemonade in summer (wonderful lemonade; she'd never again taste any so good), gulping it with an abandon of thirst which her father would certainly never have shown.

He put the glass of champagne down on the little silver tray beside him as she came round to the front of the desk. He stood up and came round the desk to her. He put his hands on her shoulders and held her at arm's length, looking into her face. She said, "I promise to obey you always." As she said the words, something inside her plummeted, something else soared. She swayed toward him, but his hands on her shoulders held her firmly upright. She closed her eyes. There was a hot darkness in her head. She stood on the brink of some black abyss where surrender was annihilating and eternal. A force from the blackness dragged her forward. She opened her eyes. He took his hands from her shoulders and she fell toward him. She rested her head on his chest. He stroked her hair. "Little Angie," he said. "My little girl." She was home, she was safe, she was his forever.

Jessica was the only person to whom she had ever told that story, years later, at university. "Goodness," Jessica had said. "It sounds positively medieval. In the nineteen fifties! Darling, what a monster he must have been."

"Oh, no!" Angie had exclaimed, horrified. "He was wonderful. The most wonderful person in the world."

She had thought she was safe forever. But ten days later he was dead.

She sighed. She opened the car door and got out. She stretched her arms.

The cottage, Jessica had told her, was the weekend place of a young London couple. It was to let because his company had posted him to South Africa for a year. "So lucky I heard about it," Jessica had said. "The one *trouvaille* of a weekend with some terribly boring people. They live quite near, but I won't be so cruel as to introduce you. I really couldn't inflict them on you." (Angie had felt the twinge of doubt that Jessica sometimes, suddenly, alerted in her. Was Jessica being sincere? Mightn't she *really* mean that she didn't want to inflict Angie on some "rather amusing chums"?) "I dashed over to have a look at it as soon as they mentioned it," Jessica had continued.

"It sounded so exactly what you're looking for. Not for *me*, really. Too cozy and snug and olde oake. But I know you like that kind of thing."

Jessica had been quite right, Angie thought now, standing on the lawn and looking at the cottage; it was exactly the kind of thing she liked. A cascade of pink roses gushed down the white wall in front of her. A small bird, wildly swinging on a spray of roses, took flight low across the lawn.

The cottage was two-storied, with a roof of unevenly faded tiles. An old brick path led between informal, crowded beds of flowers to the unpolished-oak front door. Angie went up the path, the sun blazing through her cotton shirt. She took her purse out of her leather shoulder bag and extracted the Yale key that Jessica had brought her. It really had been sweet of Jessica to do those things—seeing the owners, fixing up the lease. All Angie had had to do was to sign the agreement and arrange for her bankers to pay the rent. It had crossed her mind—Jessica was being so *particularly* helpful—that Jessica might be earning some sort of commission on the deal. Well, if she were—why not? Jessica was always chronically short of money.

She put the key in the lock and fiddled with it till it turned. As she entered the cottage, its interior coolness was in such contrast with the temperature outside that it was almost a chill. The floor was paved with bricks; that must be what gave the place its faintly earthy smell, she decided, standing in the small entrance, where two shelves of books faced the front door. She glanced at them. They were mostly paperback novels, but she also noticed several guidebooks which would help her to explore the neighborhood.

She turned to the right, into a big bare room with heavy brown beams crossing the ceiling and walls. A dart board hung on the far wall, and a group of children's paintings, bright and staring, were pinned up by one of the windows. "I told them to leave their bits and pieces," Jessica had said. "I thought it would make the place feel more lived in." In an open stripped-pine corner cupboard were old glass bottles of various shapes and sizes, greenish and semi-opaque. One window faced onto the front garden; the other onto a stretch of lawn at the back. Next to the back window was the narrow staircase with very high treads which led up to the bedrooms and bathroom. She'd go up there later, she decided. Now she went over to the white-painted wooden door in the far wall, pressing down the latch with her thumb. *Pull down the bobbin*—what was a bobbin?—*and the latch will fly open*. That was the Wolf in *Red Ridinghood*.

The floor of the pretty little sitting room, she remembered, was covered, wall to wall, with pale-gold grass matting. She wouldn't be needing the big fireplace at the moment, but she had a picture of herself in winter, sitting in front of glowing logs in the charming faded-pink-velvet armchair which was on one side of the fireplace. Facing the fireplace, a chintz-covered sofa was scattered with crocheted cushions. She crossed to the corner where the grandfather clock stood. It would be nice to get it going, but how on earth did one wind it? She should have asked Jessica, who had pointed out how a pair of hounds on one hand perpetually chased a fox on the other. "With the kill at midnight and at noon," Angie had said brightly. "Mmm," Jessica had said, and then added, "and, of course, at five past one, ten past two, quarter past three, and so on." Angie had had to spend a moment working that out. Her mind didn't move as quickly as Jessica's. She turned from the clock now to a glass-fronted box of beautifully mounted pale-blue butterflies. A labor of love, no doubt, but she didn't care for it.

She opened the door that led to a small glassed-in porch containing a wooden armchair, a small pine chest, and a stack of canvas chairs. The porch would be pleasant, she thought, on sunny autumn mornings, but at the moment it was stiflingly hot. She pulled open the glass sliding door to the terrace, where a marble-topped table stood in front of a wooden bench. A carved-stone head with heavy locks and blind eyeballs rested in the center of the paved terrace. Moss greened its cheek. She was suddenly quite sure that she wouldn't like those blind eyes staring at her whenever she sat on the terrace. She picked the head up in both hands —it was quite heavy—and carried it round the side of the porch, where she deposited it at the edge of a bed of lavender, buzzing with bees. She stood up and looked around. About ten yards beyond the terrace was the boundary fence between the lawn and the dense trees and bushes of the garden of the cottage next door. A glint of light caught her eye, and she saw that it came from the top window of that cottage, visible above the rioting green.

She went back into the sitting room and opened both the windows. She also left the door into the room with the dart board open—the whole cottage needed airing. She suddenly remembered that she must turn on the hot water, and went upstairs. The airing cupboard was in the bedroom on the left at the top of the stairs. She opened the cupboard. The switch was next to the heater, which was wrapped in a kind of quilted parka. She pushed it down and a little red light came on. Feeling efficient, she shut the cupboard and started down the stairs. Just as she reached the bottom, blackness came down over her.

It only lasted a moment. *What?* she thought, coming to, and realized that she had hit her head on the heavy beam at the bottom of the stairs. Pressing her head between her hands, she went through, past the front door, to the kitchen. She pressed the latch. Such a nice room, she thought, feeling soothed, but she was shaking. She went over to the window which faced onto the front lawn and opened it. Under the window was a long kitchen unit: stainless-steel sink, draining board, and a working surface on top of cupboards and a refrigerator. That was the other thing she must do: turn on the refrigerator. She pushed the switch, and the low hum made her realize how quiet the room had been. Again she became aware of the earth smell from the brick floor.

Next to the refrigerator was the electric stove, and next to that a large storage cupboard. The side of the room beyond the store cupboard was almost entirely taken up by a great brick fireplace —obviously never used, because there was no grate in it. A giant copper kettle hung on a chain from the chimney, and in one corner a copper jug stood filled with the papery white discs which, Jessica had told her, were called honesty.

Along the wall facing the kitchen unit was an

oak table. A bench stood against the wall behind it. On the other side, and at each end, were rush-seated chairs, each with its own crocheted cushion—someone in this house had certainly been crazy about crochet. Low over the table, a light bulb hung in a thick green glass shade.

Her head throbbed, and she realized again how tired she was. "You need a drink," she said aloud.

"A moderate quantity of alcohol," Dr. Blaumann had said, "is an aid to relaxation." Sometimes, lately, she had been aware that the amount she was drinking might not fall within that category. Often a couple of bottles a night, but always of very good wine. *("Buying good wine is one of the most sensible things one can do with money.")* But perhaps two bottles, even of very good wine, were rather a lot. She hadn't asked Dr. Blaumann about that. In fact, she admitted to herself now, she had been careful not to. Anyway, here in the country she would be free from tension. She would be relaxed. It would be natural for her to drink less.

Now she would unload the car, bring in the luggage and the stores, including the two cases of wine. She would make the bed with her own heavy linen sheets. When she had done all that, she would deserve a drink—or two.

An hour later, she was feeling much better. She was sitting on the bench behind the kitchen table—she always liked to sit with her back to the wall—drinking a glass of tepid Steinberger Kabinett 1961. She should have let it chill first, but she couldn't wait. Anyway, the rest of the bottle was now in the refrigerator, with another unopened bottle—just in case she wanted a little more in the evening. In front of her on the table were her cigarettes and lighter, a glass slipper which seemed to be the only ashtray in the cottage, and three guides to East Anglia which she had taken from the bookshelf in the hall.

How quiet it was, deeply quiet, a hush that seemed to be reinforced by the hum of the refrigerator and the buzz of a fly against the windowpane. London was never quiet like this (though surely the silence in the hall in Carlyle Square that Sunday afternoon had been *profound* —no other word for it). There she was, sinking into the past again, like a drowner, when she was determined to put all that behind her and to move, as Dr. Blaumann had put it, "in a forward direction." With her new (old) name, new (old) cottage, and her new project—which of course also had its roots in vanished days. But it was impossible to "wipe the slate," to shrug the whole weight of one's history off one's shoulders. What was important was to believe that her illness had been caused by what had happened to her, rather than by what she was. It was true that she had been ill once before (though not so very ill, and not for so long). But hadn't that, too, been because of something that had happened—

His heart had failed. He died at his desk in the library, late on a Friday afternoon. Angie was at a music lesson—Baines, the chauffeur, had taken and collected her, as usual. It was he who broke the news to her. She was glad of that. She couldn't have borne to have heard it from her mother. Though, at the same time, she despised her mother more than ever for leaving such a task to poor Baines.

The weeks passed. Food didn't taste good any more. She lost weight. She was always washing her hands—the skin became quite dry and papery. She would put out the light in her bathroom and then be sure she had left it on, and have to go back, twice or three times, to make certain.

She had to do things in a special order and arrange the objects on her bedside table in a special way. There was only one precise angle at which she could place her father's photograph so that his eyes seemed to be looking into hers. Whomever she saw first in the day, she had to be the first to say good morning, and she had to be the last person to say the words "good night" in the evening. If it went wrong, she had to start all over again. She would go back into her room and then come out again and say "Good morning" quickly, or come downstairs, say "Good night," and rush away.

At night she curled up tightly in her bed, with the light on and her eyes fixed on her father's photograph. "Little Angie, little Angie, little Angie," she would say. It had to be three times. Then she would put her thumb in her mouth (she hadn't done that since she was five) and take a small piece of the sheet in her other hand and pull at it. That was the only way she could get to sleep. Sometimes she would wake in the night, feeling that little throb she had discovered at the age of twelve. By wriggling a little and thinking of a dark rider on a dark horse, she could raise it to a tiny peak which always sank away too soon. But it was wrong to do that now. And though it was winter, she would open the windows of her room, and kneel in front of them on strings of beads which left white patches on her knees.

Although she washed her hands so often, she didn't want to take a bath, or to wash or brush her hair. And it was easier to wear the same clothes every day. She was so tired. Often she would sit by the window for hours. She didn't move at all, except to pull at the fabric of her skirt in the same way she pulled at her sheet at night.

Eventually—Angie was surprised she got round to it at all—her mother had sent for the doctor. Angie sat in her chair by the window with her hair falling over her face. She couldn't be bothered to shake it back. Old Dr. Henry took her temperature, felt her pulse, flashed a light inside her mouth, and then stood looking at her.

"Would you mind, Mrs. Maclintock, if I talked to Angie alone for a few minutes?" he asked her mother, who was hovering uncertainly in the doorway.

"Why ... yes ... oh, of course, Doctor," she stammered, backing out of the room, retreating down the passage, then coming back hesitatingly to close the door.

"What a fool she is," Angie said. There was a pause. Then Dr. Henry sat down in a chair, facing her.

"Now, you listen to me," he said. "And I mean listen, not just let what I say float over the top of your head. Angie, there is nothing physically wrong with you whatsoever. You have just got to pull yourself together. It's something that nobody else can do for you."

Against her will, her attention was captured by the vigor with which he spoke. She said, "But why should I do that when I have nothing to live for anymore?"

"Have you been seeing a lot of old movies lately? Because that's the way those words sound. Mighty foolish, especially coming from a young girl of fourteen." His tone changed. "Angie," he said more gently, "it's only natural that you should grieve for your father." He paused, and then added, rather hesitantly, "A fine man, an exceptional man." He paused again. "And just at the age when many girls tend not to hit it off too well with their mothers."

"I shall never—" she started, but he interrupted her.

"Never's a very long time. But let me get on with what I was saying. When I'm finished, you can have your say for just as long as you care to. Now, Angie, wouldn't your father have wanted to be proud of you? Don't you feel you owe it to him to make something of yourself just the same as if he'd lived? Don't you think he would have expected that? Otherwise, why would he have left you all his money?"

"Left me all his money?" she repeated.

"Well, now, perhaps I shouldn't have mentioned that, as your good mother hasn't yet seen fit to tell you." But he didn't sound apologetic. "On the other hand," he went on, "you'd be sure to find out sooner or later, seeing that everyone in this fair city seems to know all about it. Yes, when you are eighteen, Angie—not twenty-one, eighteen; doesn't that show how highly he must have thought of you?—you will come into all your father's money. That means you'll be a very rich young woman."

But that was not the aspect that interested her. "What about my mother?" she asked.

"An income for life. But she doesn't get to touch a cent of the capital." He actually winked at her. "Seems your father thought that you'd be better at handling that all on your own."

She was silent, staring down at her right hand, which ceaselessly plucked at her skirt. Now she stilled it.

"One thing I'm sure of," the doctor went on, "your father would never have given you control of that fortune if he'd believed you were going to turn into some kind of zombie. If he could see you now, don't you think he'd be shocked and surprised. In that old skirt and blouse, which look none too clean, Angie, and with your hair all hanging any which way."

She raised her head.

"So what I think is that you should just snap out of this state you're in, right now. Some people would say that was old-fashioned, that I ought to send you along to lie on a couch and tell your dreams—and pay a fortune, though that needn't bother you—to some headshrinker who'll tell you a whole lot of things that I don't think it will help you to hear. Do you want to do that, Angie?"

Emphatically, she shook her head.

"Well, then, Angie, I think you can do it yourself—no fooling! Just set down to make yourself into the kind of daughter your dad could be proud of again. Do the things he wanted you to do. And right now, as soon as I'm gone, take a bath and wash your hair, and put on a nice fresh lot of clothes."

Suddenly she felt her father's presence for the first time since his death. For the first time, really, since that afternoon in the library. She lifted her chin. She even smiled at the doctor.

"All right," she said, "I'll try."

She had finished her glass of wine. She lit a cigarette, and then got up and went over to the refrigerator. She filled her glass and, suddenly feeling thirsty, drained the contents in one gulp. She filled the glass again, and was about to put the bottle back in the refrigerator when she changed her mind and took it back to the table with her. Seated at the table, she examined the three guidebooks. Two of them looked very dull, with close double columns of type and numbered maps. The third, which had on the back a picture of the author, a poet who was also a television personality, seemed to be written in a chattier style. She looked up "Clave" in the index, and then turned to the entry, which took up about half a page.

CLAVE. This pretty village consists of a generously proportioned Lower and Upper Green, surrounded by cottages in a variety of pleasing and harmonious domestic styles, dating from the reign of Elizabeth I to early in the present century. (Fortunately, at least as far as this author is concerned, the village is undefiled by the ravages of contemporary builders.) The most significant building in the village is the 14th-century church, most pleasingly situated between the two Greens. Note the imaginative pew finials, the very early font, and the remarkable collection of monuments to members of the Donnisthorpe family. Indeed the casual visitor might gain the impression that the church is as much

dedicated to the glory of the Donnisthorpe
family as to that of their Creator.

About a mile outside the village, on the
road to Foxdene (see below), lies Fox Hall,
for more thàn three hundred years seat of the
Donnisthorpe family. The original Elizabe-
than structure was almost totally destroyed
by fire during the Civil War, when a band of
Puritans, allegedly led by the younger brother of the second baronet, Sir Piers Donnisthorpe, attacked it—Sir Piers being a strong
adherent of the Royalist cause. (Rumour has
it that the family feud then initiated persists
in another form to the present day.) The
house was rebuilt in 1665, after the Restora-
tion of the Monarchy. A stone facade in the
classical manner was added in 1758. In the
Victorian period, Joseph Paxton designed the
large conservatory, after completing the Crys-
tal Palace in 1851.

The house which contains fine paintings by
Gainsborough, Stubbs and Sargent is not
open to the public, but travellers on the
Foxdene Road will note the magnificent iron
gates by Tijou.

Those were the gates which had so much impressed her, then. She would go and have a look
around the church a little later, she decided. But
now it was so peaceful, sitting here at the table,
drinking this delicious wine, with the dazzling sun
outside and the cool dimness within. Yes, surely,
here she would be able to start again. As, after all,
she had done once before.

Baines took her to her classes: English, French,
Latin, art and music. She was sure that the univer-

sity would accept her without science and math—granddaughter, daughter, of two of its most generous benefactors, donors of the Maclintock Hall and the Maclintock Residence. But she wasn't going to presume on that in any other way. She was determined to reach the necessary standard in the arts subjects.

When she was sixteen, she started to take an interest in her father's collection of books. She pored over his old catalogues, wrote to book dealers, asking to be sent new ones. She began to love beautiful printing, handmade paper, fine bindings. But illustrated books were what she liked best: Rackham's and Dulac's especially. The first book she ordered was Dulac's *The Arabian Nights*.

At seventeen she began to taste her father's wines. She explored his cellar, read one or two books on wine. Every night she would drink one, or perhaps two, glasses from a bottle of a famous vintage. The remainder would then disappear into the kitchen. She hoped that Baines and Jane and Mrs. O'Hara enjoyed it. Her mother didn't like what Angie now thought of as "real wine." Though she was starting to sip constantly from tiny glasses of sweet liqueurs: crème de menthe, cherry brandy, or—her favorite—Tía María. One evening, Angie noticed that a new bottle of Tía María was half empty by bedtime.

Angie's father's death had tapped the flow of her mother's discontent, had opened the floodgates of her speech. Out poured the complaints—about the wasted years, about the disappearance of her youth, about the inconvenience of the house and the dangers of the run-down neighborhood. At meals Angie concealed a book beneath the table, in her lap, from which she would snatch refreshing gulps, punctuating her mother's speech with automatic responses. "With nods and becks and wreathèd smiles," Angie said to herself. Though, really, she decided, "wreathèd" was too strong a word.

How her mother bored her. Angie didn't hate her in the way she had in her early teens, but she felt stony toward her. Her mother was so futile. Hating Cleveland and its climate, why didn't she move back to the beloved South she so perpetually lamented? Or, hating the house, why didn't she get out of it, see more people, become a patron of the Symphony, or set herself up as a hostess? The truth was, Angie decided, that she had neither the gifts nor the guts to do so. *Because her will has been destroyed,* said a voice in Angie's head. But it was not a voice that Angie was prepared to listen to.

When Angie herself was the subject of her mother's fretful plaints, Angie ignored them, quietly implacable. "Don't you think you're too young to be drinking that strong wine?" It was useless to tell her that wine was much less strong than any liqueur. Burgundy, claret, even Rhine wine, tasted "bitter" to Angie's mother, and so they must be "strong," unlike the sweet drinks which she enjoyed, and which she placed in the same category as candies and desserts.

"You'll strain your eyes, poring over those old books." Yet, in the next breath her mother would ask her why she never did any "fine sewing."

"I can't think why you want to go off to Scotland—whatever your father thought about it— when you could have a much better time right here." Her mother refused to recognize that Angie wasn't having a good time at all.

She avoided her contemporaries. The gap was too great. It had been established for too long. She would much rather start again when she arrived *there*, where she was sure she would make real friends, discover others of her age who shared her interests. As her father had so often said, "Europe is civilized. America, on the other hand, is a jungle."

As she approached the age of eighteen—she would be leaving for Scotland three months after her eighteenth birthday; it was all arranged now—she knew that she must come to terms with what she thought of as "the practical side." She was aware that the practical side would always be difficult for her, for little Angie, the dreamer, the princess gazing from the window of her tower over "the darkling plain" toward the forest. But she learned to drive—that was a kind of symbol of the practical side. And she talked to her father's lawyer, her father's broker, her father's banker. (She couldn't help still thinking of them as her father's.) "I don't think I shall ever be able to understand all the details," she said. "You'll just have to explain anything very important, and then tell me where to sign." They laughed with her. She could see that they found her touching. Well, that was all right. She was sure the banker wouldn't let the others cheat her—even if they wanted to, which she had no reason to believe. They would all do what she wanted them to: leave her alone. To start her new life.

Her mother wept when she left, waltzed through a whole series of variations on the theme of loneliness. The night before Angie's departure, her mother drank nearly a bottle of crème de menthe. Angie repeated the promise she had made—to come home for Christmas. But her mother couldn't seem to take it in. She kept saying, over and over again, that this would be the last time she would see Angie, that she was old, that she was ill, that, as she put it, her death was at hand.

Angie liked Scotland at once: the old buildings, the feeling of history. She had made it clear, before she arrived, that she wanted to be anonymous, that she didn't want in any way to be singled out from the other students. She was determined that her money should not create a barrier between herself and those young, civilized Europeans. She would stay in the women's residence, just like anyone else. She would adopt all the local customs.

She suffered from the grayness: gray stone, gray faces, grayness pressing down from a sky that seemed to lie so much closer to the people, to the buildings, than the sky at home. And the cold! Certainly the winters in Cleveland were cold enough, but at least people knew how to keep warm indoors. Central heating had not figured on the list of things that her father had deplored about the United States.

She developed a definite hostility toward the little, popping, coin-fed gas fire in her room. Jeanie, the girl in the next room, was shocked by how much she kept it on. (Angie, secretly, each week, acquired a hoard of shillings from the bank, instead of fumbling in her purse like the other girls, who, if they hadn't got the right coin or if funds were low, would often just put on an extra sweater.) Frequently she would have left the gas fire on all night, if she hadn't been afraid of one of the other girls coming in. How unbearably "stuffy" they would have thought it. Quite apart from the extravagance.

None of them knew, she was sure, that she was rich. Someone once made a joke about her name ("Coming to the concert at *your* hall tonight, Angie?"). But no one made the connection. When other girls moaned over their budgets and brooded over their minuscule financial strategies, she nodded wisely, and even occasionally participated with comments imitative of theirs, though she was astonished by what seemed to her the depths of their poverty. Jeanie, a very quiet little Scots girl with frizzy hair and a luminous skin—who was, impressively, studying physics—sent her laundry home to her mother in a parcel each week, and always worked in the crowded, rustling library, both because of the free warmth and because she only used library books.

Books were one indulgence Angie was determined not to deny herself. When the other girls commented, as her shelves quickly filled, she told them that an old aunt had left her a legacy specifically earmarked for this purpose. Angie felt rather proud of this fabrication, for these upright Scottish girls accepted without question that she must stick to the terms of a bequest. Soon they stopped commenting on her purchases or even noticing them, happily unaware of the value of Rackham and Dulac first editions, of a privately printed and handbound limited edition of *Sir Gawain and the Green Knight,* and finally—most revealing of all, tucked away at the dark end of a shelf—of the Kelmscott Chaucer.

She was lucky about clothes, too. Because she

dressed so simply, no one noticed how expensive her clothes were. Once, Jeanie, glancing at a dress Angie had just taken off, had looked more closely, fingering the hem and staring at the pale-green watered silk the dress was lined with. "Beautifully finished!" she had exclaimed. "Yes, that's my mother," Angie had said. "Everything's fully lined. I'm lucky she's such a wonderful dressmaker." And Jeanie had been satisfied. But Angie had decided, all the same, not to go ahead with a dress which had been taking shape in her mind during the previous week: a dress draped across the shoulders and variously patterned in shades of brown; a dress girded with a heavy jeweled chain; a dress very much like the one worn by Mary Colwen in Rackham's illustration in *Some British Ballads*. She had recently bought the first (1919) edition—the Constable, not the Heinemann, which had appeared later the same year.

When, anyway, would she wear such a dress? She put her sketch for it away in one of the drawers of her desk—and a very horrible desk it was, she thought, frowning at the cheap veneer of its surface and its rounded, tapering legs with their metal-capped tips. She would have liked to replace that desk, but that would certainly have been noticed.

During her first term she didn't make the close friends she had dreamed of. But she took part in the coffee and cocoa parties at the residence, and she knew that the other girls felt that she was shy rather than stuck-up.

She went out twice with a serious young engineering student called Angus—once to a concert and once to the cinema. On both occasions they had drunk coffee afterward in a café, and conversation had flagged a bit. But Angie suspected that this worried her more than it worried Angus. She could see that he admired her from the way he looked at her, a way which made her feel even smaller and more fragile than usual. On their second outing, unusually loquacious, he had said, "I like to hear you talk. Your accent is so pretty." He had added, "I never imagined that an American accent could sound pretty." She realized that he did not intend that to be offensive. But didn't *she* find *him* rather a bore? she had wondered after that second date. This was a way of looking at things which she hadn't imagined herself aspiring to, especially over here, in Europe. After all, little Angie was such a timid girl. Passive she lay, waiting to be awakened by the prince. *Well,* she thought, delighted by her own sophistication, *whoever that prince is, he is certainly not Angus.*

Back in Cleveland. Snow for Christmas. Her mother sipping liqueurs. "I'm not well, Angie, and if you don't believe me, ask the doctor." She spoke to Dr. Henry. It was true. Her mother was to go into hospital on the New Year for further tests, but the prognosis was ominous. "Don't you think," he had said—dear Dr. Henry—"that you could stick around for a while. After all, she's quite alone." She had said nothing, but, a week before term began, she was gone, putting her cheek against her mother's, averting her nostrils from her mother's sour-sweet breath.

"Only ten weeks until I'm back, and, if you need me, just call. You've got the number of the residence." Running down the stairs. "Good-bye, Jane, and a happy New Year." Baines holding

open the door of the car. Inside, and the door
closed, the airport ahead. Joy!

She got up quickly from the table. She picked up
her bag and went into the hall and out of the front
door. Having checked that her key was in her
purse, she shut the door firmly behind her. Surely
she didn't have to close the windows? After all,
the church was just across the road. The sun still
blazed on her head as she went down the path.
She looked at her watch. Three o'clock. Everything was so deeply still in the heat. Standing at
the gateway, she glanced around the village. Lower Green, Upper Green—not a soul in sight. She
took the little road between the farm and the
church. She felt rather far away from herself, but,
after all, she had drunk a whole bottle of wine.
The heels of her sandals clicked on the road.

The gate into the churchyard initially created
some difficulty. She had to hold a kind of iron
clamp together with her right hand while she
heaved the gate up with her left. *Is little Angie
strong enough?* a voice asked, and she responded
caustically, "Oh, come on!" Little Angie definitely
was, and she wandered up the little grass path
that led between the graves to the church door.
She turned the round iron handle without difficulty, although it made a grinding sound.

Inside the church, it was very cool, even cooler
than in the cottage; the particular chill, the particular hush, the particular old strange smell adopted
her, took her to themselves in the way she had
always imagined was the way of old churches. Up
the aisle she wandered, toward the altar, and was
in the kingdom of the Donnisthorpes. Decorated
plaques on the wall, stone slabs on the floor. One

baronet overhead, another underfoot. Dominant, the tenth baronet, though curiously turbaned, was ideally handsome, aquiline, in marble, reclining, his chin resting on his cupped hand. She moved slowly back, down the aisle, in a dreamy slow motion, but grasping, as she passed, at the carved ends of the pews, in a kind of linked dance. Some were shaped into strange bushes, others into the forms of animals—what a dear little curled-up lamb! Some took the guise of curious heads—she wasn't sure that she liked those. But how extraordinarily solid and yet intricate the wooden shapes felt beneath her hands.

She paused, beyond the door, for a glimpse of the font. It had obviously been carved with various scenes; the divisions between them were still clear, but the figures in the scenes had been worn away, were just rough and rather disquieting shapes. She moved, with excessive haste, toward the door, glanced back, felt the pulling gaze of the tenth baronet. She turned the handle urgently, was glad to be out of the church, in the bright sunlight. Though the sun had sunk noticeably lower in the sky, the heat seemed as powerful as before, and her body welcomed this after the chill of the church. Her head was feeling a bit swimmy; she was suddenly aware that she wasn't walking quite straight. She was glad there was no one about. She hoped that unseen people weren't watching her from behind their windows.

Nearly home now. She fumbled with the key. It took her several tries to turn it successfully. Then, at last, she was safe inside. She headed for the kitchen, opened the door, and stood quite still. The green-shaded light above the table was turned on. It shone down on the stone head that she had moved from the terrace to the bed of lavender. The head lay exactly in the center of the table, with its sculptured locks, its greenish cheeks, its sightless orbs. She picked up the full glass of wine on the table and downed it. How could it taste so vile? The last thing she was conscious of was those round blind eyeballs.

TWO

She awoke, came to, recovered, to find herself sitting slumped in the chair at the head of the table. What? Where? She sat up, forcing her eyes wide open, then sank back, closing them again. When, after a moment, she reopened them, it was to acknowledge the truth: the head had gone, the light was off. There was nothing on the table but an empty bottle and a glass, the guidebooks, and her cigarettes and lighter. Her hand shook in the air. She forced it down, flat on the table. A breath that she had gulped in she leased slowly out. Then she lit a cigarette.

Back to London. That was the first thought. *Back to Blaumann* was the second. A hallucination. For what else could it have been? Yet, in her mind's eye she saw it so exactly: locks, narrow mouth, eyeballs. In the pool of light under the green shade. She stood up and switched on the lamp. Yes, surely the light had fallen in just that way. She paused, and then turned and hurried through the house, through the glassed-in porch, onto the terrace and round the side of the cottage. There it was, exactly where she had put it—at the edge of the border of lavender, over which the bees still avidly buzzed and circled.

What was the time? She looked at her watch. Twenty past five. Which meant that she had been asleep (unconscious?) for about two hours. Because she distinctly remembered having looked at her watch and having noticed that it was three o'clock when she set out for the church.

She sat down on the wooden bench on the terrace, rested her elbows on the marble table, and cupped her chin between her palms. Back to London. Having failed. Blaumann: "I thought that perhaps you were not quite ready." Jessica: "Poor old Angie! So you couldn't even stick it out for one day?" Driving back to London, driving away from the future, driving back into the past. And driving, specifically, where? To some hotel. Desk clerks, waiters, chambermaids. People to whom she must express choices about rooms and menus; people to whom she must give money, and to whom she must issue instructions.

"How long will you be staying?" "I'm not quite sure." Something funny about that. They would look at her more closely, might even recognize her—a face that had been in so many newspapers —even though nearly two years had passed. And then the whispers, the furtive glances, perhaps a tip-off to some gossip columnist ("Arriving alone, wearing blue jeans, at Brown's Hotel last night . . .").

Driving. That was really the worst prospect, feeling as she did now. The pressure building up inside her, her wrists stiffening, her hands clenched in a rictus on the steering wheel. Till all she wanted would be to let go, turn, bury her head

in her arms on the back of the driving seat, and
. . . *let it happen.*

No, she must pull herself together—a memory
of Dr. Henry—and she must wait until tomorrow
before doing anything at all. She must work out
what had actually happened—as opposed to what
she *imagined* had happened. After all, she had
drunk a whole bottle of wine, she had been out in
the hot sun, and—yes, of course—she had hit her
head on that beam. Taking all those things into
account, together with the rather strange feeling
that old church had given her and the great dislike
she'd taken to the stone head in the first place,
wasn't it really only *natural* that her perceptions
should momentarily have been distorted? A picture of the head in the pool of light suddenly
recurred, again so vividly. But she shut it off, blink-
ing sharply, as if clicking a viewer on to the next
slide. Which was, surprisingly, a still life of food.
A chunk of bread, a piece of Brie, a few slices of
Neapolitan salami. She hadn't had a single thing
to eat all day, she realized. Which was a further
explanation of that . . . mirage. Yes, she must eat.
And, to help the food down, she'd have a glass or
two of wine. Something red would be comforting.
Burgundy. The 1961 Clos de Tart. That would be
good for her.

And it was. She ate half the loaf of French
bread, eight slices of salami, and a big piece of
Brie—really, for her, an enormous meal. The burgundy was wonderful. When she had finished the
bottle, she positively floated around downstairs,
making sure all the windows and doors were
closed but not worrying about a thing. Then she
went upstairs.

The upper story of the cottage had a circular

feeling. On its own, at the top of the stairs, on the left, was the bedroom with the water heater in it. But the other rooms all opened out on each other. Facing the stairs was a small bedroom which led into a large cupboard space, almost a room, containing a chest of drawers and a rack for clothes. From the other side of this cupboard-room, a door opened into the main bedroom. On the right of the stairs was the bathroom, and this also led to the main bedroom, with a tiny passage, paralleling the cupboard on the other side.

The main bedroom was low-ceilinged and whitewashed, with a double bed covered with a patchwork quilt in pale prints and faded velvets. She drew the sprigged cotton curtains, and the early-evening sun filtered through them into the white room, which was like a cool cave, she thought, a cool white cave. She felt pleasantly tired now, though not terribly sleepy, in spite of the wine, and she put on a white cotton nightdress and lay down between the white linen sheets.

It would have been nice to telephone someone, she thought suddenly. But, as Jessica had explained, installing a telephone in this part of the village would have meant extending the telegraph wires and would have taken a long time to arrange, and, if she needed to telephone, there was always the call box outside the pub. All the same, perhaps she should try to get a telephone put in. But whom would she phone? Jessica was the only person she could think of, the only person she was at all in the habit of calling.

She had seen both Jessica and Richard for the first time, on the same day, in the Kenmare Café, during her second term.

The passage that led from the glass-paneled door, which opened onto the street, to the interior room, which housed the café, was painted a deep coral and lit by a ceiling lamp in a yellowy parchment shade. It was this warm, glowing effect that had attracted Angie, struggling up one of the many steep hills of the town, late one afternoon, her fingers freezing inside her woolen gloves and her feet numb in spite of her fur-lined boots. THE KENMARE CAFÉ, she read, written in Old English lettering, and underneath that, COFFEE, TEAS, LIGHT MEALS AND SNACKS. She knew immediately that a cup of coffee, vile though it would probably be, was the thing she wanted most in the world at that moment. She pushed open the glass door, moved, rather hesitantly, down the passage, and entered a large room, lit by dim candlelike lamps on some of the tables, which gave it the un-expected, rather exciting look of a restaurant—or even of a nightclub, Angie thought, though she had never been inside one. She went to the nearest empty table at which she could sit with her back to the wall, sat down on an absurd little gilt chair, and looked around her.

There were not many people in the café. The time was twenty past five, in the lull between the afternoon's Teas and the evening's Light Meals and Snacks. Two women in stiff little hats were talking in low voices. At another table, an elderly, vaguely clerical-looking man crouched over a book, cramming fragments of cake into his mouth with a kind of desperate negligence. She became aware of the approach of a waitress, in a black dress and a white muslin apron, who now extended a menu toward her. "Oh, just coffee," Angie said, and added, "please." As the waitress was entering this order punctiliously on a docket, a sudden wild, high-pitched female giggle made Angie turn her head. At a table to which she had not previously directed her attention, a young man and a girl were sitting. They seemed, from their closeness, to be bound in the light from the lamp on their table, like participants in a seance. The girl—the only possible possessor of that abandoned giggle—was facing directly toward Angie. Her little head was framed in a high collar of some soft fluffy white fur. Her green eyes glittered like Christmas-tree frosting. Seen that first time, laughing fiercely in her frame of fur, Jessica had looked to Angie like some wild princess from a Russian fairy tale. But it was the man on her right who then held Angie's attention. The upward glow from the lamp illuminated his face like a perfectly placed spotlight. His beauty, its extreme blondness enriched by the lamplight, seemed to Angie so extraordinary that she sat literally gaping at him. It must have been an awareness of this that caught his attention; his large eyes were suddenly fixed on her, rested for a second, but were not held, and moved back to the face of his companion. But Angie was in the grip of an obsession.

From that day, Angie began to haunt the Kenmare. She started to drop in for either morning or afternoon coffee (not both; she made that a rule) every day. She would take a book, to occupy herself when he wasn't there and to use as cover when he was. Which was two or three times a week. She became accustomed to the sudden hollowing of her stomach when she saw him. Somehow it was a little worse when he came in after she did. When she arrived, she was always taut for the shock of his presence. But, if he wasn't there, she would relax a little after the inevitable let-down and start to read her book, though not usually taking in very much of what she read. Every time someone came in, she looked up, but somehow she was never prepared when it was he. Always it was like going up a floor in one of those attendant-operated store lifts. Up lurched her stomach, and down, quickly, went her eyes, to the page at which her book was open.

Sometimes he was with other people, sometimes with the girl with whom she had first seen him, an extremely striking girl, though she never made quite the same impression—so fierce and wild—on Angie as she had the first time. Very occasionally he was alone, glancing round restlessly, drinking his coffee quickly, and then leaving immediately.

Once, as an experiment, Angie took Isobel, a hefty-legged third-year law student who lived on her corridor, into the Kenmare with her. They were passing the door. "Come and have a coffee," Angie said, regretting the invitation as soon as she uttered it. Isobel looked up at the Kenmare sign and whistled. "Very posh," she said. "You must be in the money!" As Angie went through the door, holding it open for Isobel to follow, she was already mourning her lost privacy, the opportunity it afforded her to concentrate in silence on the whole range of emotions—hope, dread, lurch of exhilaration, slow diffusal into resignation—which were her daily lot in the Kenmare.

He was there, and with the girl, Angie noticed as she entered the room. "Let's sit here," she said to Isobel, leading the way to her usual place, with its good view both of the door and of the table where he sat.

Isobel flung herself down in the chair next to Angie. The waitress came over at once, smiling at Angie, who, however, turned quickly toward Isobel, not wanting the waitress to say anything that would make her status as a regular customer apparent.

"Coffee?" Angie asked hastily. "And wouldn't you like something to eat? I've just had a surprise postal order from home," she added, to forestall any financial demurs.

"Oo, *well*, if you're *sairtin*, I'd just love a wee cream scone."

"Two coffees, one cream scone," Angie said.

There was a pause after the waitress had gone, and then Isobel said, "You see that laddie over there?"

"What laddie?" Angie asked vaguely.

"That one, over *the-er*." Isobel's voice sounded twice as loud as usual as she pointed unmistakably at the table which absorbed all of Angie's attention.

Responding absolutely reflexively, Angie put a hand on Isobel's arm and said, with urgency, "*Sssh!*"

"Whatever's the matter?" Isobel was asking, *fortissimo*, when fortunately she was distracted by the arrival of her cream scone, which immediately became the focus of her interest. "Oo, doesn't it look *grand!*"

Angie poured the coffee. As Isobel settled into her scone, Angie said, in a tone so quiet that surely anyone—even Isobel—would be bound to lower hers in response, "You were saying? About that young man on the other side of the room?"

(Surely, if she identified him so clearly, Isobel would not feel the need to point again.)

"Oh, him. Yes"—and blessedly the volume was much reduced—"he goes to my jurisprudence lectures. Good-looking, isn't he? But awfu' toffee-nosed. His name's Richard Charteris, and he's always making jokes in the lectures, but the prof doesn't seem to mind. He's certainly got a nerve," she concluded, returning to the remnants of her scone—there was a blob of cream at the corner of her mouth—and leaving Angie to digest her feast of information.

It was later that day that Angie had her vision of clothes. She started to make sketches of them, in ink and wash. They were in soft pale colors. They floated. They flowed. They embodied panels of embroidery and old lace. They were, in those days, original, and that had made her afraid. But she found the name of a dressmaker, in *Vogue,* and at half term she went up to London. She bought fabrics and old embroidery and seed pearls and lace. (And at the same time she bought a tapestry, wall hangings, and two Persian rugs.) She took the materials to the dressmaker and told her that she wanted three dresses and three cloaks. The dressmaker, an elderly Frenchwoman, at first studied the mass of materials with astonishment. But after Angie had shown her her sketches, she said, "Yes, I think I understand what is in your thoughts. It is ... the fairy-tale princess, *la belle au bois dormant,* but in a modern time." And Angie nodded her head. She dreamed her way through the fitting. Her arms were lowered and raised; she was moved a pace forward, a pace back; her head was turned from side to side. "You'll send them to me by post?" she said, when all the measuring was finished. "But mademoiselle will surely want another fitting." "No, I can't manage it. You've got all the measurements. Surely you can get them right," said Angie in a tone she had never used before. But the dressmaker still seemed doubtful, though she murmured that she would do her best. "Shall I pay you now?" Angie asked, taking her checkbook out of her bag and watching the dressmaker's face light up. "Tell me the amount, and then, if you can let me have the things quickly, in about a week—the dressmaker gave a little exclamation of horror—"I will send you an extra hundred pounds. And," she added, "I will have other things made in the future." It was all arranged. Hailing a taxi to take her to Euston, getting into it, settling back in the seat, she was amazed at the way she had behaved. She suddenly remembered the story of the Red Shoes: *"Dance you shall! You shall dance in your red shoes till you grow pale and cold, till your skin shrinks and your body is like a skeleton!"* She shivered, but then a wave of wild exhilaration swept over her, and she laughed.

The new clothes arrived ten days later. She took the parcels into her room and locked the door. She swayed and turned in front of the mirror in the pale dresses and the rich cloaks.

She studied her face. Then she went out and bought the palest foundation cream and powder. She bought pale-green shadow for her eyes and a black pencil to outline them: nothing for her cheeks, nothing for her lips.

The next afternoon, she put on the least startling of the dresses. It was of very fine white wool, banded with turquoise ribbons. Over it she wore a cloak of black velvet, which she fastened at the throat with a silver brooch. She painted her skin and her eyes and released her hair from its ponytail, and brushed it a hundred times, and went out to the Kenmare.

People stared at her, but she didn't care. She ordered coffee from the astonished waitress. She knew he would come in, and just as she was finishing her coffee, he did. He sat down at his table and looked around the room. His eyes rested on her, and this time they did not move on. And she met his gaze levelly for a long minute. Then she signaled the waitress, and paid her bill, and left the café.

She had decided that this must happen three times. A week later she would wear the dress of pale-green silk with the embroidered panels, and over it the dark-green velvet cloak. And the week after that she would wear the pale-gold dress, sewn with seed pearls, and the cloak of glowing amber.

But she didn't need to. Two days after what she thought of as her first appearance, she was standing in the town's main bookshop, looking at a book of poems. She glanced up. He was facing her across the table of books, and looking straight at her. "The Pale Lady of the Kenmare," he said. A voice in her head answered: *And with those words her fate was sealed.*

She wanted, overwhelmingly, to take what he had said back to her room, and brood over it and play with it, and try it this way and that, like one of her dresses. So she closed the book and put it back on the table, and made her way out of the shop. As she opened the door, he said, behind her, "Hey, have I offended you?" and she couldn't help being sorry because she felt that this particular scene had ended with the words "The Pale Lady of the Kenmare."

But of course she turned round. "No, of course not," she said. "Good. Where are you off to?" he asked, falling into step with her, outside. "Back to the women's residence," she answered. "I'll walk with you. I'm going that way," he said.

As they walked, he asked her questions—her name, where she came from ("You're American?"), what she was studying. It was curious to be talking to him—or, rather, answering his questions—after having lived with the idea of him for so long. She had a momentary sense of disappointment. Seen close, his lips had a petulant, pouting look, and his eyelids flicked up and down as he talked. And wasn't there a stiffness about him, under all the ease, a kind of rigidity? But as they came nearer to the residence, these impressions faded from her mind, and gradually his face resumed the exact form of that perfect face she had first seen in the lamplight.

She was answering in monosyllables, and as they reached the gate, the conversation was dying away. "Well," he said, "I must hurry. Late for a lecture, as usual." She broke in, "Why don't you come to tea one day? Next week." (Time for anticipation.) "This time next week," she continued. "Before your lecture." He was looking surprised. A little reluctant? But he said, "Oh, yes. By all means. I'd love to, of course."

During the week, she bought two old Waterford glasses and four Worcester plates, which she found in an antique shop, a bottle of claret, a bottle of Martell Cordon Argent, two tall red candles, two boxes of black Russian Sobranies, a box of Turkish Delight, four ounces of Beluga caviar, and—because of the caviar—a bottle of Stolichnaya vodka, all of which she put away in the bottom of her wardrobe.

She realized that she had been remote from the other girls lately, but only because she was so preoccupied. Now, however, she was rather glad, because her room was becoming so full of things that she didn't want them to see. And the last thing she wanted was some great hockey player, such as Isobel, bursting in during Richard's visit to the Pale Lady of the Kenmare.

She was up early on Thursday morning. First she cleaned the room. Then she rolled the Persian rugs out from under the bed and spread them on the floor. She covered the bed and the wicker armchair and her horrible desk with the embroidered wall hangings. She fastened the tapestry on the wall above the desk. When she went out to her first lecture, she locked the door behind her.

Everything was ready long before four, when she expected Richard. She was wearing her second dress, the green one. She had done her face, and had brushed her hair two hundred times.

All the food and drink was arranged on the desk, with the plates and glasses and two nickel teaspoons she had extracted from the residence dining hall. (She'd forgotten to buy anything to eat the caviar with, and it was too late now.) She drew the curtains; the Northern dark was already descending, and by the time Richard arrived it would be complete. She lit the candles and put five shillings in the gas meter. Then she sat down on the Persian rug in front of the fire.

The knock made her jump to her feet—could she have fallen asleep! "Yes," she called. "Come in." And he was in her room, peering around in the dimness. "I say," he said, and then again, "I *say.*" It was an expression she'd never heard anyone use in real life before, and it reminded her of certain British childhood books of her father's which, years ago, she had picked up, glanced at, and rejected. But he had regained his self-possession. "What an amazing room," he said. "Really astonishing."

"I'm glad you like it," she answered, though of course he hadn't really said that. "Can I give you some claret?" she asked, going over to the desk.

"Claret? At *tea time!*" he exclaimed. A silence fell.

"It's very nice claret," she said after a moment. "Or there's some brandy, if you prefer that."

He was over by the desk now, too, peering at the bottles in the candlelight. "*Very* nice claret," he said. "Yes, I'd love some. Let me," he said, taking the corkscrew from her hand. He was nifty with a corkscrew. "You'll have some, won't you?"

"Oh, yes, please," she said, and laughed. He laughed, too.

He handed her her glass of wine, and raised his, and she knew he would say "To the Pale Lady of the Kenmare," but he didn't. He said, "Oh, is that Turkish Delight. Turkish Delight and claret—what could be more splendidly decadent than that? Come on. Let's have some."

She refused the Turkish Delight. The thought of it with the wine made her wince. But he ate one piece, and then another, very quickly.

"Do sit down," she said. He sank down in the armchair, and she perched on the edge of the bed.

He had an amazing flow of small talk. The time

flew. She refilled both their glasses, and later offered him a third.

"Yes, that *would* be nice. What a tiny girl you are," he said as she stood up. "Little Angie."

The words "little Angie" had a sudden, shatteringly erotic effect on her. But now he was kneeling by the bookcase, running his fingers along the backs of the books, and then, from the darkest corner, carefully extracting the Kelmscott Chaucer.

"*What* a nice book," he said, turning the pages, pausing to look at one of the Burne-Jones woodcuts. "Where did you get this from? What a very splendid book to have."

"Er . . . I bought it," she said.

"Did you now? With your own pennies out of your piggy bank. What a *very* clever girl." The book was back in the shelf, and he was on his feet again, taking his refilled glass from her hand. "Goodness," he said, "*I* shall be Titus."

"Titus?" she asked.

"Titus the Emperor, ha ha ha." And when she still looked blank he added, "Tight, you know—plastered."

"Oh, I see," she said. There was another pause. Which he broke by saying, "But, seriously, I must rush away now. My lecture, you know. Glug, glug, glug, it will have to be; and what a pity with such a delicious drink."

"Oh, I'm sorry." She had forgotten about his lecture. "I'd thought we might have some caviar and vodka later."

He roared with laughter. "What an outrageous girl you are! Please let me—as you people say—take a raincheck. Yes? Take a raincheck till next Thursday? Would that be all right?" And when

she had nodded, and as he put his empty glass
down and turned to the door, he added, "And, oh,
could I bring a friend? Or, rather, a cousin. Well, a
friend *and* a cousin, actually. You'll love her," he
continued. "Everybody does. She's called Jessica.
Next Thursday, then? And thank you so much for
all the gorgeous tuck." He was gone.

In the distance, a dog barked. In the bedroom, the
light was dying. The whiteness was draining from
the walls.

"But what a gorgeous room, and what an amazing
dress you're wearing!" Jessica was everywhere at
once, exclaiming, smiling, suddenly reminding Angie, this time, not of a Russian princess but of
Rackham's picture of the cat who persuaded
Venus to turn her into a woman. (A mouse scut-
tled across the room, and out of bed the woman
leaped from beside her startled lover.) Jessica's
little head turned this way and that on her long
slim neck. There was something about the propor-
tions of her face—the shortness of the nose with
its firmly cut nostrils contrasting with the width of
the cheekbones—that had an addictive effect on
the beholder's eye. And over and above the fascination of this architectural riddle was the surface lure of her smooth, textureless, creamy skin,
the glint of her slightly slanted, frosted eyes, and
the brilliant gloss of her lips.

"Richard told me about all your lovely things—
your marvelous books." Jessica's eyes darted along
the shelves. She pounced, pulling out the Rackham *Alice's Adventures in Wonderland*, turning
the pages. "No, it's no use; I'm wedded to the
Tenniel illustrations. Give me a child before the

age of seven, and he's mine for life, as the Jesuits say." *Alice* went back on the shelf. Then, just as Richard had, she dived for the Kelmscott Chaucer. "Yes, my goodness ..." Jessica's eyes met Richard's, then flicked back to Angie.

They ate the caviar. They drank the vodka from three little eighteenth-century cordial glasses Angie had bought that morning—that there were three of them in the shop had seemed to her a good omen for the afternoon. "*Za vashe zdorovye!*" Precisely, Jessica raised the glass. Back she tossed its contents with one quick movement of her wrist. Richard and Angie followed. Angie choked; it was the first time she had ever tasted a neat spirit. They all laughed. Angie felt a hectic flush mounting in her cheeks. Jessica's pale color never changed, however fast she tossed back the little glasses of vodka. All the time, she laughed and chattered.

Richard was quiet that afternoon. Not subdued; rather, more relaxed than Angie had seen him before, nodding, laughing as Jessica held the stage. Till suddenly he was on his feet. "My lecture. You must forgive me if I dash."

Jessica said, "Oh, Richard, how devastatingly conscientious of you. *I* can stay, though, can't I, Angie?"

"Of course you can." Angie was so pleased by this request that she found she didn't really mind Richard's departure.

"Shall we have another lovely vodka?" Jessica asked.

"Do, please. I don't think I could. Though I wouldn't mind a glass of wine."

"Oh, yes, that would be *much* nicer," Jessica said at once.

Angie went over to the table for the bottle of Chateau Montrose. "Nineteen-fifty-two," she said. "Not as good as the 1953, but rather nice all the same."

Jessica burst out laughing. "Angie, you're quite amazing," she said. "Such expertise. So unexpected from an American."

"My father was very interested in wine," said Angie, a little coldly, carefully pouring the Bordeaux into their glasses.

"Tell me about your father," Jessica said. So Angie did. It must have been partly because of the vodka and wine, for she had never talked in this way to anyone before. They sipped the wine. Angie refilled their glasses. The gas fire hissed gently. Jessica sprawled elegantly—Angie noted that it was possible to do that—in the armchair. She had kicked her shoes off. Her feet were long and narrow. And Angie, sitting on the floor, her feet crossed under her, staring into the orange and blue and white gas jets, talked. Jessica seemed to draw it all out of her, like a magnet. The house in Cleveland. The money—"But don't tell anyone." "Darling, not a soul." Her mother. Her father—"What a monster he must have been." "Oh, no. He was wonderful. The most wonderful person in the world." Jessica had raised her eyebrows, pursed her lips, then shaken her head and shrugged her shoulders. "If you say so, Angie. And now tell me—what do you think of Cousin Richard?" Haltingly, Angie murmured, "Well, I'm not sure." "Nonsense," Jessica had replied, "I can see you think he's quite delicious. Don't you? Admit it. I'm the very essence of discretion." And then, not waiting for an answer, "I know he's very taken with *you*." "Do you really think so?" Angie had asked.

"Darling, I *know* so. I know absolutely everything about Richard. We've been inseparable since infancy."

"Really," Angie said.

"Mmm, he practically lived with us in Scotland. His mother's terribly poor, but terribly brave—a widow. And though, heaven knows, we're poor, too, still there was country air, good plain food, and all that. Much better than being cooped up in a poky little London flat. And when he was with us, then Aunt Cecily could go and stay with people."

"Stay with people?"

"Yes, in the country, and so on. To save money." Jessica said it matter-of-factly. But, *poor Richard*, Angie thought, *what a terrible childhood*.

"Anyway," Jessica continued, "all her old chums rallied round to send Richard to a proper school. But he usually came to us for the holidays. Though I wasn't always there. Sometimes I went to my mother, in France."

"Your mother lived in France?" Angie probed uncertainly.

"Yes, my parents are divorced. My mother's been married three times. She's got a villa in Nice. Drink, drugs—you name it. And terrible young men. Waiters, and so on, you know?"

Angie nodded dumbly.

"I used to keep it all from Daddy, of course. But, really, staying with her was quite an education."

Angie broke the silence. "And then you and Richard came to the university together?"

"Mmm. Because Daddy's so broke, I went to the local high school—me being a girl, it didn't matter, really. But then I won this scholarship here, and, as it was all *free,* Daddy thought, why not? It was partly because of that that Richard came here. Anyway, Oxford and Cambridge are so much more expensive. And full of temptations to extravagance and sin—I'm sure that's what Aunt Cecily thought—for a poor boy like Richard. And I think she believed I'd be a good influence on him. Imagine!" Out came that high, uninhibited giggle that Angie had heard in the Kenmare. "Though you should see me at home in my shaggy skirts and jerseys, with my clean, shining face. Not *entirely* me. Though I'm not quite sure what is, really."

And now she was standing up, sliding her feet into her shoes. "Must go. I've stayed and stayed. Have you been bored to death?"

"Oh, *no!*" Angie protested truthfully.

"Sweet of you." With her fingertips, Jessica lightly tapped Angie's cheek. "Soon!" she said.

Lingering, seated, by the fire, Angie had thought about Jessica. How sophisticated she was! What an amazing friend to have made! And then she had wondered, was it really true about Richard? Could he really be—how had Jessica put it?—"terribly taken" with her?

It had seemed it must be so. For, from that very day, Richard had started to court her. Well, what other word was there for it?

She had been sitting at her desk, next afternoon, writing an essay, when there had been a knock at the door. She was wearing a gray woollen dress. The rugs and hangings had been put away. "Come in," she had called, expecting it to be Jeanie or one of the other girls. But it was Richard.

"Hmm," he said, looking round, "much tidier," and then, seeing her expression, "well, different, anyway. Less of the mysterious East, yes? I thought you couldn't always live like that. And I knew you didn't always wear the Lady of Shallot kit." He looked her up and down, smiling. "Do you ever wear tailored things? You know, suits and so on. Tweed. With . . . shoulders." He sketched these absolutely square shoulders by moving his forefingers apart horizontally. "Rather military. As opposed to the sort of slope-away Pre-Raphaelite thing. No? I just wondered." His eyes went down to her feet—she was wearing low-heeled dark-blue shoes, which emphasized their smallness. "Boots?" he asked. She looked at him mutely. "D'you ever wear boots? I love boots—especially black ones, with high heels. And those shoes with very high, sort of spiky heels are nice, too."

She must have looked idiotically bewildered, for he burst out laughing, then broke off the laugh abruptly in mid-spate, as it were. "Don't know why I'm talking about your clothes. Because you look very very nice as you are." (He pronounced "very very" *vey vey*.) "It must be because I'm interested in your appearance, I suppose." And he added, on a soft, low note, "Hmmm?" And then, when she didn't answer, "You're a very quiet little girl today." She smiled radiantly. He frowned. "Little one?" he said, as if testing the words. The warm shiver that ran through her left a ripple on her body. Almost with a shrug, he half turned his head away. "Got a cup of tea for me?" he asked. "A real cup of tea this time, not a glass of claret."

She laughed. "No tea, but I have some coffee."

"You have some *caw*fee? I adore your funny accent. Well, coffee will do for now, but if I'm going to come and see you often, you must get in some tea. A nice powerful Darjeeling. And crumpets to toast in front of the fire, and so on." He extended himself on the rug, leaning on one elbow and holding an imaginary toasting fork to the fire.

She went down the passage to the room where the students could make tea and coffee and do their ironing. When she came back, he was still lying on the rug. She brought his coffee over to him, and he took it from her, leaning on one elbow to spoon in the sugar. He put the cup down on the floor, and suddenly subsided flat on his back. "Would you like to stand on my chest?" he asked. "Stand on your chest?" she repeated foolishly. "Yes, to test my amazing tummy muscles. Just look at them!" Indeed, through his checked viyella shirt, she could see a solid, hard plateau, extending from his waist right up his rib cage. "Come on," he said, patting the plateau encouragingly. "Oh, I couldn't," she said, "I might hurt you." He looked irritated, so she started to remove one shoe. "No, no, don't take your shoes off. Quite unnecessary."

He extended his right hand, and, hesitantly, she took it in her left; and, slowly and tentatively, she put her right foot on the wall of his diaphragm. Then, swaying a little, she gently brought up her left foot beside it. His eyes were closed now. "You're very light," he murmured in a rather fretful tone. "Try shifting about a little. Jump up and down, if you like."

"Oh, no, I couldn't," she said, letting go of his hand, and stepping carefully back onto the ground. He sighed and opened his eyes. He got up. He was standing, almost touching her. He bent forward and kissed her. She closed her eyes and went limp against him. He put his hands on her shoulders to straighten her, and continued to rest his very soft lips against hers. She opened her eyes. His were open, too; they were, she noticed, a very light bluish gray. Then he stepped back, picked his coffee mug from the floor, and quickly drank its contents. "I must go now," he said. "See you soon. In fact, why not have coffee with me and Jessica at the Kenmare tomorrow? Eleven o'clock?" She nodded. She had a lecture, but she decided to cut it. "Eleven o'clock," she affirmed. "Well, good-bye—little Angie," he said, and was gone.

She went over to the window, realizing that she would be able to catch a glimpse of him leaving. She parted the curtains and peered into the dimness. In the light from a streetlamp she could see snowflakes falling. There he was. She could see him as he emerged from the front entrance. He stood still for a moment, under the lamp, in the snow. Suddenly he raised his arms in a wide upward gesture, abruptly halted in mid-air—the gesture, she recognized, of a conductor urging his orchestra to a climactic chord. Then his arms flopped to his sides, and he was off down the street, running. In a moment the evening had absorbed him.

She turned away from the window, went over to the armchair, and sat down. So much to think about. First and foremost, of course: The Kiss. Her first, and not quite what she had imagined— but what had she imagined? That wasn't clear. And there were those other things to wonder

about: the standing on his chest; and all that talk
about boots and square shoulders. Smiling, she
shook her head.

She had had no idea that he was trying to shape
her into something he would be capable of endur-
ing.

When she woke, the room was full of light. She
looked at her watch. A quarter after eight. She
couldn't remember when she had last slept so well
and for so long. She got out of bed immediately—
something else she never did these days. For ages
now, getting up had been a matter of gradually
preparing herself to meet the day—always, however, huddling down first, to try to recapture the
night. When that failed, there was the first cigarette, usually stubbed out half smoked and followed by another retreat down into the bed-
clothes. Hopeless. So then the second cigarette,
after which her hand would stretch out for whatever book was on the bedside table. But she usually found she didn't feel like reading. So then the
slow progress toward sitting on the side of the
bed, looking at her feet, until she finally dragged
herself off to a further postponement—a long hot
bath. By that time a great chunk of the morning
would have been nibbled away, which, of course,
had been her intention all along.

But not today! She was over by the window,
pulling back the curtains, putting her head out the
open window. There was still dew on the grass,
and three guinea fowl were pecking at the ground
under a tree on the lawn. She dressed quickly,
putting on jeans and a shirt. In the bathroom she
brushed her teeth and washed her hands under
the tap, splashing her face with water. Then down

the stairs she clattered in her sandals, remembering the beam just in time. Opening the window in the kitchen, plugging in the electric kettle, getting out the coffee beans and grinder, she was possessed by an extraordinary exhilaration. Thank heaven she hadn't gone back to London yesterday (driving away from the future, driving back into the past). What a stupid thing that would have been to do, just because of the combination of a little bit too much wine with that famously overactive imagination of hers. "Silly Angie," she said to herself, but quite fondly.

She was *hungry*. Hungry twice in twenty-four hours! There were eggs and bacon among the supplies she had brought from London. An egg and one strip of bacon would have been a good lunch for her, usually—breakfast was never more than a piece of toast. But now she fried two eggs and three rashers. How delicious it smelled, and how vividly good it tasted. Sitting back afterward with her second cup of coffee, lighting a cigarette, she explored the prospects for the day ahead. Should she start work immediately? No, she decided, she'd wait till tomorrow, would take one day off, to settle down, to become acclimatized. She'd do the dishes, and then go for a stroll round the garden, get to know her territory, her kingdom. After that, she'd finish unpacking, make the bed, take a quick bath. And then she'd go for a drive round the neighborhood, look at some of the old villages, before having a lager and bread and cheese in a pretty little pub, perhaps the one here, on the Upper Green. After lunch ... well, she'd think about that later. She certainly had a full morning mapped out.

The dishes done, she lit a cigarette. She went

out through the front door, leaving it open behind
her. The air was warm and fresh; she could feel
that it would be hot later. She closed her eyes and
rested her back against the wall of the house.
With her eyes shut, she became aware of various
sounds: the buzzing of an insect; the voices of
small birds; the distant, absorbingly erratic purr
of a dove. The sun was warm on her eyelids. She
was suddenly conscious of a distant roar, growing
louder. She opened her eyes, which were dazzled
for a moment, just in time to see a large black car
flash past, beyond the grass verge. What a pace to
go at on such narrow country lanes! The sound of
the car receded in the distance—along the road
she had taken yesterday, she supposed. She
stretched, yawned, and looked around her. On
either side of the path that led to the gateless
gateway were the cottagey flowers and a little
stretch of lawn. She turned right, past the kitchen
window. A bed of herbs grew against the wall of
the house, and three low steps led down to the
lawn at the side where she had seen the guinea
fowl that morning—no sign of them now. She
rubbed a sprig of thyme between her fingers as
she went round to the back of the house. An easy
garden to keep up, she thought, looking at the
grass, broken occasionally by a fruit tree or
shrub.

Beyond the lawn, on this side, were low bushes
and high, uncut grass. At the back the lawn ended in a hedge, beyond which lay a field of ripen-
ing grain which gave a pleasing feeling of space.
It was a pity the terrace didn't have a more open
view, she thought, as she went round the other
side of the house. The trees beyond the fence did
grow so very thickly, and seemed so near, but,

anyway, they would keep the terrace sheltered. Again, light glinting on the window of the cottage beyond the thicket caught her eye. She wondered who lived there. It would be nice to have a pleasant next-door neighbor to call upon in an emergency. *There aren't going to be any emergencies,* she told herself as she went past the porch. "Is the horrible head still in its bed?" she said aloud, making a charm of it to raise her courage. There it lay, in the lavender. She turned the corner of the house, passing the car, parked neatly in front of the sitting-room window. She needed a new packet of cigarettes, and she was sure there was one on the dashboard. Yes, she was right. Opening the packet, she went into the house.

She couldn't resist having some more coffee. She heated it and took a cup out onto the terrace, which the sun had just reached. The day was getting warmer all the time. How she loved heat. Sunlight out of doors and good heating inside. A source of contention with Richard. Though contention hadn't really been the word, at the beginning.

Just as, previously, she had tried to create herself for Richard in the form of an image that was in her own mind, so now she falteringly groped her way toward embodying his declared preferences. Everything changed; the engine struggled, with jerks and shudders, into reverse. Neat little suits were ordered from a tailor. A shoemaker measured her for a pair of boots. She put on lipstick ("You look so ghostly with no color in your face except that green eye stuff"). She even had her hair cut and set.

She stood at the edge of damp fields, with a

Hermès scarf tied under her chin, watching him stagger or roll about in the game called rugger. She went with him to the races, where she backed the horses he suggested and tried to show some interest in whether they won. She accompanied him to his favorite Western films—more horses, but at least the cinema was warm.

Often, very often, Jessica was there; interpreting, explaining, advising. Obedient herself to the tribal customs, she was always ready to giggle about them with Angie, was never pompous in the way that Richard could be when Angie questioned some deeply held belief. ("But *why* can't one wear a college scarf?" "Because it simply isn't *done*.")

Jessica at the races: "If you don't enjoy it, look at it as a delicious painting—a darling Stubbs." Jessica at a Western: "It's a *ritual*, darling. With fantastic homosexual undertones—just like rugger." And, "Really, Jessica, what utter nonsense you talk," Richard would say, but smiling, not in the least annoyed. He never minded anything that Jessica said.

But there were times, of course, when she could not rely on Jessica.

"Little Angie, silly girl," he would murmur, and she would dissolve. But the problem was that it was only things he said that made her feel that way. Nothing he did made her feel it. She didn't feel it when their mouths touched, or when he ran his hands vaguely over whichever parts of her were nearest. She certainly didn't feel it when, on the rug in front of the fire (usually turned down too low nowadays, because Richard found her room too hot), he would shut his eyes, his lips would get a swollen look, and he would mutter,

"Lie on top of me. Press down hard. I want to feel your *weight*." She just felt silly. For surely it was he who should be lying on top of her, pressing her down, crushing her, crushing little Angie, who would then—wouldn't she?—murmur and moan and melt. *The knight would carry her into the night.* No, it was never at all like that.

It was in the summer term that Richard asked her to marry him. Her third term and his last.

She had left Cleveland a week early at Christmas; it was retribution that she should have to return there a week early at Easter. Her mother was dying. How could anyone have changed so much in eight weeks? It was as if something had eaten her away from inside, and then thrown her down, a bundle of sticks and skin, on the hospital bed. Dr. Henry was cold. He blamed her for not having stayed, at least to play the role of witness. If not that role of daughter—loving, grieving—which she, and perhaps he, knew she would never have been able to perform.

"Angie," her mother said, "I want you to start all over again." What could she mean by that? Angie felt a flash of the old impatience. Out came her mother's claw-thin hand across the sheet. She took it in hers and her mother died.

Start again? That was just what she found she couldn't do during the weeks that followed. This was the time, she knew, for severing the material bonds. She must pension the servants. She must arrange for the house to be sold (developers were clamoring for the site, for office-building). She must visit the banker, the lawyer, the broker. She must concentrate on their speeches about transfers and taxes and capital gains.

But she found herself, day after day, in the library. She told the servants she was not to be disturbed. She took volumes from the shelves and piled them on the desk in a great circle. Held in that circle, she sat in her father's chair, sipping his wine, turning the pages of one book after another.

She had sent Richard a postcard, to his mother's flat in London W8. She received a rather stilted letter expressing his "deep sympathy" with her in her "terrible loss." "I can understand," he wrote, "as the only child of a widowed mother, just what this must mean to you."

Should she write again? What he said was unreal to her. Wasn't *he* unreal to her? Was anything real except the great chair in which she huddled, the great circle of books, the bottle of wine?

But, late one night, long after the servants had gone to bed, she had opened a new bottle of wine, and when she had drunk half of it, she had suddenly gazed around her, at the wall of books, lit by the desk lamp, and the darkness and stillness beyond. She had cried, and then she had poured out how lonely she was, how sad, how trapped, in a long letter to Richard. When she went to bed, she left the letter on the silver salver in the hall.

She woke late next morning, and the first thing she thought of was her letter. She must get it back. But Baines had already mailed it.

After that, she received three letters from Richard in quick succession. "Dear little Angie," the first began,

* * *

What a sad letter! You do sound strange and your writing is very wobbly!

I think of you so much and hope that you are feeling better now. You must come back soon and not sit there brooding.

London is v. dull at the moment. No one I know is about except Jessica who is doing some ridiculous job in a flower shop behind Harrods, because she is broke—me too! She sends you her love.

Of course I miss you, you silly girl. Why do you need to ask. Anyway I am sure I shall be able to convince you of the fact as soon as I see you again! Shall it be oysters and champagne? Oysters will still (just) be in season. (Ten days to go until the month gets an "r" in it!) You must fly to London (soon as possible) and *not* go straight to Scotland. For one thing, I should like you to meet my mother. I have told her so much about you. (Don't be frightened! She is not at all alarming! Indeed she is a marvelous person, so kind and brave. Everyone loves her and admires the way she has coped with all her difficulties in life.)

The other reason you must come to London is because of me! There are so many things I want to show you and places I want to take you to.

Let me know.

> Lots of love from
> Richard
> xxxxx

She carried the letter around with her, reading it again and again. But two days later, another letter came.

Late at night

Darling,

I have just reached home and I am thinking of you, my fierce wild girl. I am seeing your head poised threateningly above me, and I am running my finger along the stern line of your lips. Don't be too angry with me—will you?—darling, that is, not *angrier than I can bear*. Or I might be too frightened at the prospect of our next meeting!
I can feel your feet now, your feet that tread so strongly. I see your head flung back, your firm arm upraised. Shall I ever be able to persuade you to pity me, or will you remain adamant, however much I beg and plead?

Do you really demand that I should admit I deserve whatever treatment you mete out to me?

Yours,
Richard

What could he mean? She read the letter again: "the stern line of your lips . . . angrier than I can bear . . . your firm arm upraised . . . whatever treatment you mete out to me." None of it seemed to make sense. It didn't sound as if he were talking to her at all. How could she answer it? But next morning there was another letter—special delivery, with a red EXPRESS label on it.

Darling little Angie,

This is written in wild haste. The truth is I can't think what I said in the letter I wrote to you the day before yesterday.
The fact is I went out with some chaps I was at school with, and got—I'm forced to admit it—TITUS. Tighter in fact than any emperor I've heard of, except old Nero, perhaps, when he was fiddling away while Rome burned.
Anyway, I'm sure what I wrote was all complete nonsense. So just forget about it, won't you. Cable me when you will be arriving.

Love from
Richard

XXX XXX

Oh, well, she'd always read that being drunk made people behave peculiarly. She threw away the strange letter—though she kept the other two —and deliberately erased it from her mind. And that day she made appointments with all the people she had to see, and also booked her flight to London. "Start all over again"—her mother's words came into her mind.

She arranged for everything to be sold except her father's books and his desk and chair, which she had shipped to storage in London. His wines she had delivered to Dr. Henry (he had a big house, with a basement). She wrote him a note thanking him "for everything you have done for us all."

She knew that she would not return.

*   *   *

It was spring in London, fine but windy. Richard took her to Kew and to Syon House and to Hampton Court, and they walked in Kensington Gardens, up and down the Broad Walk and round the Round Pond. It was nice to do all those things, and it was particularly nice to be out because, whenever she was in it, Angie was filled with longing to escape from Richard's mother's flat. It had a small dark dining room, and a crowded little sitting room (drawing room, Richard's mother called it) with a settee (sofa) and armchairs that were too big for it and were covered in a floppy pinkish beige material. Signed silver-framed photographs of important people, about whom Mrs. Charteris ("Call me Cecily, my dear") told long stories, were massed on spindly little tables. Smudgy watercolors, and one dark, heavily varnished oil of two dead birds, were suspended on long wires from brass picture-hooks on a rail high on the wall. The room was claustrophobic, but also very cold, Angie found, in spite of the fine weather. Richard's mother switched on the electric heater when she saw Angie shivering— "But I *insist.*" And then, shaking a playful finger, "You Americans and your central heating! It's quite weakening, I'm told, and terribly bad for old furniture, of course. Though I suppose all the furniture is new out there." Was she stupid, or rude? Angie was not able to make up her mind about that, though she had made up her mind, at first meeting with Cecily ("Why, what a *little* thing she is, Richard!"), that she couldn't stand her. Despite her softly waved gray hair, and her pastel makeup, and her soft skin, Angie thought she had one of the hardest faces she'd ever seen,

even though it bore a disconcerting resemblance
to Richard's.

She had wanted to stay in a hotel. But no—"I
insist." So Richard slept on the pinkish beige settee (sofa), and Angie was given his tiny dark
bedroom, which looked out on a sort of tiled well.
There were photographs of school teams on the
walls, and a one-eyed teddy bear glared hopelessly down from the top of the wardrobe.

The oysters and champagne never materialized,
and Angie was too tactful to suggest providing
them herself. However, on the last night before
she and Richard went back to university, she did
manage to persuade them to come out to dinner
with her at a place Cecily suggested, where huge
pale portions of steamed fish (*steamed* fish, even
if it was turbot!) were the specialty ("In England
we say spec*i*ality, my dear"). With parsley sauce.
Anyway, Cecily couldn't prevent her having fun
with the wine list (which, to her surprise, wasn't
at all bad), though Angie learned, weeks later,
from Richard, that this had shocked Cecily deeply
("The man should always choose the wine"). And
apparently, on the same principle, Angie should
have secretly pressed the money for the bill into
Richard's hand before they left the flat, instead of
paying it, herself, in the restaurant. (Though
Richard laughed when he gave her this information, she had the feeling Cecily's opinions were
perhaps not so very different from his own.)

When they got back to the flat that evening: "A
drink?" Cecily suggested with unusual alacrity
(she was normally rather slow on the draw in this
regard, Angie had noted, lingering on the American phrase with a particular relish). Diving into a
cupboard, Cecily produced an unopened bottle of

cognac. "Oh, no thank you, Mrs. Charteris." "Now, how often have I told you that you must call me Cecily." "Cecily, I mean. I'm sorry, but I never drink spirits." "Now, just a drop—I insist. Richard, pour Angie a drink. Not for me," she added hastily. "I'm off to bed. So many things to do in the morning. Now, don't keep Angie up *too* late, will you, Richard? Good night, Angie, my dear. Good night, Richard."

There was something about this precipitate departure which seemed to embarrass Richard as much as it embarrassed Angie. He picked up a china shepherdess from the mantelpiece and then put it down again. "Are you *sure* you wouldn't like some brandy?" he asked. "Yes, quite sure," she answered. "Well, I think I will," he said, and poured himself a substantial dollop before coming to sit down next to her on the settee. He drank the brandy very fast, put the glass down, and pounced on her with a kind of desperate ferocity, pushing her backwards, pressing his mouth down hard on hers, fumbling with the zip at the back of her high-necked dress. Wasn't this ardor what she had been missing? No, it wasn't. She was suddenly quite sure of that. "Richard," she exclaimed very sharply, pushing him away from her. Startled, he released her, and drew back. "No," she said emphatically, speaking to herself as much as to him. "Definitely not."

He was not offended; that was certain. On his face there was a curious smile. Gentle, was that it? No, not quite that. But now he was kissing her hands with soft little kisses. He tilted his head back to look at her. He was still smiling in that indefinable way. His extraordinary good looks startled her, for perhaps the hundredth time. "I

must go to bed," she said. "Just as you like, darling
Angie." How sweet he was. Wasn't she lucky to be
loved by someone so handsome and so sweet?

It was a question she often asked herself during
the term that followed. And always she knew that
the only possible answer to it was yes. Just as yes
was the only possible answer when, two weeks
before the end of the summer term, he asked her
to marry him.

She drove along the road she had arrived by the
day before, passing the ruined cottage and the
great iron gates. She drove along the narrow
lanes, taking detours through small villages, opening the doors of little churches and looking inside,
but not, for some reason she didn't analyze, going
in. Twice she stopped at small antique shops; in
one she bought a blue and white Staffordshire
creamer shaped like a cow. Most of the time, she
just drove, enjoying the sun and the country, but
enjoying even more the sense that she was free.
She wasn't sure that she'd ever really felt free
before.

It was after one when she got back to Clave
and parked the car outside the Fox and Hounds.

THREE

The Fox and Hounds was a low whitewashed building with a square graveled space for cars in front of it. On the left of this square was the village hall, a single story of red brick. At the edge of the road, on the right, was the freshly painted scarlet public call box. Behind this a small wooden gate in a white fence led to a patch of lawn on which there were three round white tables and several plastic chairs. One of the tables had a bright umbrella screwed into it, improbably, in this context, advertising Pernod. Centered, at the edge of the gravel near the road rose the inn sign, on a tall white post. The fox had, at least temporarily, outwitted his pursuers. With flamboyant brush and blandly grinning mask, he lounged in the foreground, in a clump of bushes. In the distance hounds and a single horseman streamed across a field.

No one was sitting outside, and Angie went into the pub. The bar (there was only one) was a low-ceilinged room with walls darkened by smoke to a yellowish cream. There was a dart board on one wall, and various notices of local events. Otherwise, the furniture consisted of wooden tables and benches and a few rather forbidding-looking wooden chairs. An old man in a cloth cap and a very long overcoat was sitting in one corner with a pint of beer in front of him. There was no one else in the room, but as Angie approached the bar counter, the landlord came in from a room at the back. He had a drinker's grayish purple skin, blotched and veined. The hand which placed her half pint of lager on the bar shook with a small but persistent tremor. Drink can eat you away like cancer, she thought, and disliked the idea.

"Lovely day," she said.

The landlord turned his watery gaze toward the front window, as if he felt it necessary to verify this. "Yes," he said, and nodded. "Yes, it's a fine day."

"Do you have any bread and cheese?" she asked.

He shook his head. "No food, miss. 'Cept on a Saturday. There isn't the demand for it." Continuing to shake his head, he disappeared through the door at the back of the bar.

Angie took her drink over to a table under the back window and sat down on the bench behind it. Outside the window was a small vegetable garden. Beyond it a German shepherd dog paced about a wire enclosure. As it turned at each end, the chain it wore clanked. Watching the dog made her feel restless, and she swiveled round to face the room again, wishing that she'd brought something with her to read. At that moment, an old Rolls drew up outside the front window. A minute later, a woman and two men came into the bar, which immediately seemed crowded.

The woman and the man directly behind her were both very tall. But where the woman was bony, gawky, somehow horselike, he was quite simply the best-looking man Angie had ever seen. Dazzling. If a dark person could dazzle. Then she realized that it was his eyes, which, astonishingly in that darkness, were brilliantly blue. (The woman's eyes were brown.) Over them arched and quirked very black eyebrows, and his hair was so black that the gray in it showed up as white. How old was he? In his late forties, she guessed.

She suddenly realized that she was staring. Gripped by the same kind of visual obsession that had seized her in the Kenmare—all those years ago. But next to this man's, Richard's remembered blond beauty seemed insipid. Here was the dark knight of her dreams, no longer faceless. But really, that was too much! She could imagine what Jessica would say: "A fantasy fuck, darling?" Jessica's language had coarsened. And what was disconcerting was that every time she said one of those words, in her clear high voice, it sounded newly coined. "Oh, Jessica!" Angie had once exclaimed. "It's extraordinary what a Puritan you are," Jessica had said coolly, "and, like all Puritans, seething with sex under the surface." "Oh, what nonsense," Angie had exclaimed sincerely. For *all that*, she had felt with a shiver of distaste, was over for her now. It was so much nicer to be alone in a white cotton nightdress between white linen sheets. *White as Snow White after she had eaten the poisoned fruit. Till the dark prince came riding through the forest.*

The man who came last into the pub was a strange figure. He was hardly taller than Angie herself. He had pointed features, like an elf. Even his ears appeared slightly pointed. He had shiny little gray eyes and a cockatoo crest of whitish blond hair. Although he must have been as old as the dark man, he was wearing very tight jeans and a vermilion T-shirt.

"Charlie!" the dark man called. From that one word it was evident that he had an upper-class voice of the most extreme kind, the first syllable being pronounced *chull* and the second being a rendering of the German "ich" raised to the kind of singing hum usually employed to call a distant dog. Chullich needed no second summons, but hurried in from the back. "Ah, it's you, sir. Sorry if I kept you waiting. How are you, sir?" "Oh, very fit, thank you. But you look as though you had rather a rough night, what?" Evidently expecting no reply to this, he turned to the woman. "What are you having, Ven?" She and the second man had seated themselves at a table in the middle of the room. "Pink gin for me," said the woman. Upper class, too, but crisper. "Woody?" said the dark man. "My usual crimson joy, please, Peregrine," shrilled the elf.

Chullich, having prepared the pink gin, was now opening a bottle of tomato juice. A bloody Mary? But no—there was no sign of vodka. Angie was surprised. Woody didn't look like a teetotaler. "And a big gin and tonic for *me*," said the man called Peregrine.

It came over her in a rush. The antipathy. The voice, the affectations. "Big" instead of "large," which was what ordinary people said. The stress on "me." How they loved themselves. How they hugged themselves to themselves; they were their very own darling teddy bears. "*I* think so" and "one for *me*" and "who's been sleeping in *my* bed?" The answer to the question, in her experience, being almost anyone, but preferably of unorthodox sexual habits and inferior class. Nothing like something *low* for getting the adrenaline flowing. Deliciously aware that Mummy would disapprove, and so would Nanny, too!

They were all sitting at the table now, talking in low voices—that, at least, was unusual. Anyway, she must leave. What was the point of sitting here, getting stirred up about *Them,* the very people that she'd managed to get away from. Certainly she would have to give this pub a miss if, as seemed obvious, these people were regulars. She was picking up her bag when Peregrine leaned toward her and said, "It's making us sad, seeing you all alone there. Won't you come and sit with us?"

"I was just leaving," she started to say, but he was standing up, had lifted a chair from another table and deposited it between his own and the woman's, and had fixed her with those astonishing eyes. And a blast of charm, a positive gale of it, raised her off the bench and landed her there, in their midst.

"My name is Peregrine Donnisthorpe," (that sounded familiar—why?) he was saying, "and this is my wife, Vanessa. And this is George Ashwood, who is known as Woody."

"Yes, Woody to all and George to none," said the elf. There was a pause.

"I'm Angela Maclintock," she said. At one time she had thought of changing her name completely, but had decided against it. Very few people remembered her maiden name. They all thought of her as Angela Charteris. That was what the papers had called her.

"From America, I think?" Peregrine said.

"Yes, though I've been in Britain quite a long time now."

"Well, Angela," Peregrine said, "what can I get you to drink?"

She hesitated. "Perhaps half a pint of lager."

"Oh, you can't go on drinking that depressing, watery stuff. Why don't you have some gin?" ("Some" gin, not "a" gin, Angie noticed.)

"Oh, I never drink spirits," she said, and added, "I usually only drink wine."

"Mmm, well, I admit that the prospects for that are poor at the Fox and Hounds. Sherry is the answer. Chullich has quite a reasonable dry sherry tucked away somewhere." He got up to order it before she could either accept or refuse.

"Terribly bossy, Peregrine," Vanessa said, smiling at Angie and showing a lot of large and rather chaotic teeth. Not for the first time, Angie wondered why They never spent any of their money on orthodontics. But the smile was rather endearing. It had a sort of hockey player's keenness about it. What she couldn't understand, though, was why these people were being so nice to her. She didn't *look* rich, not even to an eagle eye, in her blue jeans and peasant blouse. If Peregrine had been alone, he could have been trying to pick her up, but not, surely, with his wife present. And they weren't drunk—drink could occasionally lead to indiscriminate bonhomie, hastily contracted out of once sobriety returned, she had noticed. She remembered some wretched couple whom Richard once, when "terribly Titus," had invited for a drink next day, and how extremely rude he'd been to them when they turned up.

Peregrine put the glass of pale sherry on the table in front of her and sat down.

"And what are you up to in these ever so rustic parts?" asked Woody.

"I'm staying in the village. Down on the Lower Green. I've taken a cottage there," she said.

"Oh, the end one," said Peregrine. She nodded. "I heard those weekend people had let it," he went on. Then, "All on your own?" he asked. Perhaps he *was* trying to pick her up. She couldn't help feeling intrigued by the idea. He was "such a dish," as Jessica would have said. Angie smiled.

"Mmm," she said, "I'm alone," and, feeling she had to give some kind of explanation (though why?), "I'm trying to write a book."

"Don't tell me," Peregrine said. "Let me guess. It's a novel. A novel about the adventures of a sensitive young American girl in the decadent Old World."

"No, I'm no Henry James," Angie said, laughing.

"Henry James . . . Henry James," Vanessa said, trying to place the name. "A sort of ghost story, wasn't there? Tremendous goings-on with a valet and a governess."

"Yes, indeed. A very ill-regulated household," said Peregrine. "*The Turn of the Screw* is what you are talking about, Vanessa."

"That's the thing. *The Turn of the Screw*," said Vanessa in a pleased voice. "The ideas seemed quite good, you know, but I couldn't really get on with it. He had such a roundabout way of putting things."

"Such, I believe, is the critical consensus," said Peregrine, smiling at Angie, who giggled, but then looked anxiously at Vanessa, not wishing to offend her. However, Vanessa appeared delighted at what she obviously considered a tribute to her literary acumen.

"But we still don't know what *your* book's about," Peregrine said. "You are proving evasive, distinctly evasive."

"You ask an awful lot of questions," Angie said.

"A habit I acquired during the war. I was in Intelligence."

"Anyway, it's only a children's book," Angie went on. "A collection of fairy stories. And I'm illustrating them myself," she added.

"How super," Vanessa said. "How long have you actually been in England?" she asked. She had a curiously uninflected voice. Something about it made Angie feel sure she was tone deaf.

"Five years," Angie said. "Well, four in England. I spent one in Scotland. At university."

"Only one year? You were sent down?" Peregrine asked with lively interest. "What for?"

"Nothing so dramatic, I'm afraid. I got married."

"Ah?" A question hovered, unspoken.

"I'm divorced," she said, answering it.

"You'll probably find it dreadfully dull in Clave," Vanessa said. "Dreadfully dull place for a young girl on her own."

"You must come to see us when you get too bored," Peregrine said. "We live very near here. Just outside the village, really. On the Foxdene road. Fox Hall, the house is called. Big iron gates."

"Oh, yes," Angie said "Donnisthorpe. Of course. All those tombs." There was a pause. "In the church, I mean," she added.

"As you say, all those tombs. But not in the house, I promise you. So you may visit us without fear. Why not now, in fact? One more drink here, and then back to Foxers for a bite of lunch. Good idea. Ven?"

"Super," said Vanessa, the teeth reappearing. She seemed all keenness. And Woody chimed in, "I've got ever such a splendid soup simmering on the range." He broke into song: "*Soup home on the range, where the peer and the cantaloupe play. Women for children, boys for pleasure, but melons for delight, as the Arabs say.*"

"Woody is our jester," Peregrine said.

"The scourge of the court, my dear," Woody bubbled. "Old cap and bells, that's what they call me."

"But are you sure?" Angie spoke to Vanessa. Why were they being so nice to her? Perhaps, she told herself, she really had become paranoid. Why shouldn't they just be nice people? Country people were probably quite different from those London ones. More friendly. And pleased to see a new face.

"No prevarication," Peregrine said. "It is arranged. But one more drink first."

"Terribly bossy, Peregrine," Vanessa repeated, again with that great grin. Really, she seemed to have as many teeth as the Wolf in *Red Riding-hood*.

By the time she had drunk her second sherry, Angie was feeling pleasantly hazy. When they got up to leave, she realized that the old man in the corner had left without her noticing. "Good-bye, Chullich," Peregrine called, and Chullich hurried from the back of the bar, to touch an imaginary forelock.

Outside, on the gravel, Angie started to move toward the Porsche.

"Your car? Nonsense," Peregrine said. "Though I admit it's a very pretty car. But we shall bring you back to fetch it. Now, Woody shall drive us all. Our ever sober chauffeur."

"Some of us don't need the drink to be cheerful," Woody interposed saucily. "Not like others, as I could name," he added, bouncing into the front seat of the Rolls. Peregrine opened the front door, and Vanessa got in. "You shall sit in the back with me," he said to Angie, opening the door for her.

The big car glided smoothly down past the church to the Lower Green. Angie felt as if she should be waving to a loyal populace. She smiled. "Joke?" Peregrine asked, but she shook her head. He shifted in his seat, and rested his arm on the backrest above her head. She was acutely conscious of its being there. Now they were turning off, along the Foxdene Road. As they rounded a sharp bend, Woody pressed the horn. It played the first five notes of "John Peel." It seemed only a moment before they were passing the ruined cottage. "I wonder why someone doesn't do something with that cottage," Angie said.

"Mine," Peregrine said. "Falling to pieces. I keep meaning to put up a notice saying that it is neither for sale nor to let. Damn people from London keep coming to ask about it. Last thing I want is to have them parked on my doorstep. With their gnomes," he added. "No, rather let it rot."

The great iron gates were on the left now. "We don't use that entrance any more," Peregrine said. "Those gates haven't been opened since Queen

Mary came to tea. I remember my father putting all his favorite furniture in the attic. Under dust sheets, too, in case she had a whim to go up there. She was famous for admiring things. And when she did, of course, people felt they had to give them to her."

They took a turning to the left, which Angie hadn't noticed before. The lane ran along beside a high wall, with trees showing over the top of it. They came to a five-bar gate between red-brick posts with stone pineapples on them. "Tradesman's entrance," Peregrine said, getting out to open it.

When they had driven through, and he had got in again—once more flinging his arm along the back of the seat—they drove within a colonnade of trees. They seemed to drive a long way—farther than the drive from the village to the turning off. Then suddenly, they emerged into a great circular sweep of gravel. Trees bordered it, in a semicircle, with another, wider drive emerging from them. Facing this was the house, of golden stone, with a pillared porch topped by a balustrade. Built onto the side of the house, on a lawn, the great glass conservatory was like an elongated onion. As Woody drew up in front of the door, with a crunch of tires on gravel, Peregrine gripped the nape of Angie's neck, so suddenly and fiercely that she nearly called out. A shudder ran right through her. He let go, the car stopped, he was out of the car and round in front of the porch, opening her door and then Vanessa's. Angie stepped onto the gravel, which she saw was overgrown with little weeds. A sudden raucous cry made her jump, visibly. Everyone laughed. She turned her head, to see a peacock, tail spread, picking its way toward them over the gravel. "Oh," she exclaimed, delighted, "What a beautiful bird!" She moved toward it. It turned aside, again giving its harsh cry. "Not really a pet," Peregrine said, opening the front door, with its great knocker in the shape of a dolphin.

Vanessa and Woody went in. Peregrine held the door open for Angie to follow them. Peregrine was smiling, and she realized that her hand was on the back of her neck, exploring the place where his hand had gripped her. She felt a blush flood over her face, and she snatched her hand away and lowered her head as she went past him, into the house.

Woody bustled away at once. "I must see to my soup. Followed, I *think,* by an omelette with chives and a nice green salad. There's a bit of Brie, too, that I bought in Bury yesterday. . . ." His voice died away down a corridor as he hurried off, reminding Angie of the White Rabbit in *Alice in Wonderland.*

"Super cook, Woody," Vanessa said. "I loathe cooking, myself, so of course I'm frightfully bad at it."

"But an ace with a tool box," Peregrine put in. "Ven completely rewired the house a couple of years ago. I'm hopeless at anything like that. Almost as bad as my father. When the electricity was first put in, he wouldn't even touch a switch himself. There was a little boot boy he would always summon to turn on the lights. He had an extraordinary faith in that boy's command of electrical power. 'He's the only person who understands it,' he used to say. It annoyed our old butler tremendously."

They were standing in a very large hall. The

floor was stone flagged, but the whole central area was covered by a huge carpet with birds and flowers on it. The hall was dominated by a great central staircase, leading to a gallery. On the walls on both sides of the hall, pictures were fitted into every foot of space, like pieces in a jigsaw puzzle. Drawings and sepia sketches, watercolors, little and large oils. Landscapes, horses, dogs, pictures of flowers and fruit. Portraits, historical scenes—she noticed a Shylock, exaggeratedly Semitic, cringing before an extraordinarily arrogant Antonio. Dominating them all, at the top of the stairs, was an immense portrait of a tall, beautiful woman in a black riding habit. She held a riding whip. From her pale face, piercing blue eyes gazed coldly. Her lips were firmly set. Her hair was closely coiled around her head. These coils, and the length of her neck, made Angie think of snakes. "She has eyes like yours," Angie said to Peregrine. "But she's much more frightening than you are."

"Hmm, don't be too sure of that." He smiled, then added, "My mother. By Sargent.

"We'll have a drink in the library," he went on, "and then I might show you something of the house."

"Oh, yes, I'd like that," Angie said.

The library, which opened off the hall, was painted dark red. Chairs and a sofa were grouped around a fireplace. Vanessa flung herself down on the sofa and picked up a copy of *The Times*, which was lying on the floor. "Vanessa's favorite reading," Peregrine said. "Births, Marriages and Deaths. Vanessa is interested in the essential things."

Vanessa looked up. The teeth appeared. "I like to keep in touch," she said.

"One used to look at the marriages," Peregrine observed. "Then one used to track down which of one's chums were giving birth." He paused. "Now I'm reaching a stage at which more of my acquaintances are to be found among the dead."

"Oh, Peregrine, how morbid you are," Vanessa exclaimed.

A desk covered with papers stood facing the French windows, with a dark-red high-backed armchair drawn up to it. Outside the windows, beyond overgrown lawn and bushes, was a rose brick wall, broken by a round, columned arch.

The library was walled with glass-fronted bookcases, containing rows of calf-bound gilt-lettered volumes. "You collect books?" Angie asked.

"Unfortunately," Peregrine said, "I am in a situation where I tend, rather than augmenting my ancestral possessions, to have to dispose of them. When the entail permits, that is. Which is rarely."

"At least things are preserved for your children, then," Angie said.

"I have no heir. Or rather, I should say, my brother is my heir. The gray sheep of the family. He is a don. Or, rather, a professor. Of sociology, if you can imagine anything so undignified. At some red-brick institution in the Midlands. He has two unwashed and bearded socialist sons. I prefer not to contemplate the future of Foxers."

He was pouring drinks from bottles on a silver tray. He handed Angie a glass of sherry and poured gin for Vanessa and himself. "Bring your drink with you," he said, "and we'll wander round a little." Vanessa stayed in the library, the paper close to her face. Angie suddenly wondered if her lips moved as she read.

In the dining room, on the other side of the hall, four places were laid at the top of the great mahogany table, which had twelve chairs ranged around it. Woody must be kept busy, Angie thought. She wondered if he did all the housework.

They crossed the hall again and went down a flagged corridor behind the library. At the end of it a glass door opened into the conservatory. Tropical plants grew round the sides, in beds edged with white stones. Other plants stood on tables. In the center was a goldfish pond into which a little fountain played. Next to the pond stood a life-size statue of a black woman on a pedestal, holding a cornucopia of fruit. A great bamboo chair was beneath the statue, and other chairs of ornamental white wicker, twisted into rosettes and curls, were dotted about.

"It's a dream," Angie said.

"Yes, I'm extremely fond of conservatories. The Victorians adored them. People were always kissing each other in conservatories in those days," he said. He was standing very close to her, looking down at her and smiling. "Rather fun," he said, and turned toward the door. She was blushing again.

Back in the corridor, he opened another door, and they went into a huge ballroom. The paintings of clouds and cherubs on the ceiling were so blotched with damp that they were almost indistinguishable. Packing cases, some open, some closed, stood around the walls, interspersed with little gilt chairs. A vast chandelier, with many of its lusters missing, hung from the center of the ceiling. Directly under it stood a large mechanical musical box, inlaid with art nouveau scrolls. Behind a mesh, she could see an arrangement of castanets, triangles, a drum, and little spikes like hedgehog's prickles. On top of the musical box was a hand-printed notice: ONLY TO BE PLAYED BY P.P.D.D. BY ORDER. "Who's P.P.D.D.?" she asked.

"Me," he said. "Peregrine Palfrey Devonwood Donnisthorpe"

"How does it work?"

"You wind it up, or rather I do, because other people always overwind it, and it plays twelve tunes. Seven waltzes and five marches. I shall show you after lunch."

The sound of a gong, booming, filled the room. In the hall, Woody was striking it with enthusiasm.

The soup was delicious. Though it was such a hot day, there was a touch of chill in these huge, high-ceilinged rooms. Peregrine kept opening bottles of a drinkable claret. Angie lost count—was it three or four? Woody was drinking apple juice, and by the time they had finished their omelettes and were eating the Brie, Angie was happily, dizzily vague. She was laughing a great deal and gazing at Peregrine, but Vanessa didn't seem to mind.

After lunch they went into the ballroom, and Peregrine wound up the music box and started its mechanism. As it began to play the "Merry Widow Waltz," he took her hand.

He waltzed absolutely in time, round and round, never reversing, till her head was spinning. She didn't know how she was still standing; she would have fallen without his hand, so firm at the base of her spine. She rested back against it and, head back, let herself gaze into those brilliant eyes. Everything around her blurred. There were only the eyes. Then the music stopped. "Splendid," said Peregrine. He released her. She swayed. "Waltzing is such excellent exercise," he said.

She gulped. "Excellent," she agreed.

In the cottage, that evening, it seemed very quiet. Woody had driven her back late in the afternoon. She had wished it were Peregrine who was driving her. Now she remembered that sudden grip on her neck, and shivered and smiled, sitting on the terrace, with a glass of hock in front of her, and the evening coming down, and two white moths drifting past, circling, as she had circled in the decaying ballroom.

What an amazing day. And how sweet they had been to her. Quite different from those people Richard had spent his time with, even though Peregrine and Vanessa were upper class and probably had backward ideas—"unwashed, bearded socialists," and so on. But they were fun to be with. Something she had never felt about Richard's friends. Or, really, about Richard.

They had been married on the last day of June. In church, in an abundance of roses. She had had a feeling of haste, of pressure, of being rushed along. She had felt it ever since they became engaged. "Let's get married soon," Richard had said. He had been offered a job in an office in London, arranged by one of Cecily's old friends. There was nothing to stop their getting married— except the fact that she had two more years of her university course to complete. But: "Oh, Angie darling, why on earth do you need a degree? You can read all the books you want to in London. And you can go on with your sketching, take lessons from someone or other. In fact you'd probably be able to spend *more* time than you do now on the things you really like." And, once she had consented, she had been whirled away—parties, dances, weekends in country houses, visits to ancient relations of Richard's, appointments with dressmakers. Till there she was, going up the aisle, shrouded in lace, on the arm of Richard's godfather, with Jessica behind her, wearing a green that was just the color of her frosted eyes, and Cecily, in lilac, in the front pew.

The hotel reception. A buzzing crowd of Cecily's old friends. So many people Angie didn't know. Shaking hands, longing for the blessed moment when she could drink some of the Krug 1955, which Cecily had thought such an unnecessary extravagance—Angie, however, had stood firm. After all, she had thought, I'm paying for it. And had been immediately ashamed of such crudity.

Changing into one of those "little suits" she hated—pale blue with a close-fitting hat of tiny feathers. One night at Claridge's, Richard and she drank so much champagne that she really couldn't remember anything next morning. Except that she was sure that, as she put it to herself, "nothing had happened."

The honeymoon was spent in Antibes—chosen after some debate. She had wanted to go to Italy, but wops and heat combined were apparently too much for Richard. The South of France, however (in spite of heat and frogs), was more acceptable.

Perhaps because of some Edwardian concept of "the Riviera"?

She in white chiffon, white *broderie anglaise*, white silk; a series of nightdresses, each more delicate, more ultrafeminine, than the last; and each, as she would realize later, more unappealing to Richard. They rolled about in her single bed, sweating, he apologizing angrily, blaming the "ghastly heat," but really, she couldn't help feeling, blaming her.

It was on the fourth day that he gave her the black raincoat. In the morning they had walked around the old town. They had visited the Picasso museum, which she had enjoyed, but which had bored Richard, and then eaten lunch under a tree in a beautiful square which was entirely filled with little restaurants. She had liked the food; Richard hadn't. They both drank a lot of wine. After lunch they went back to the hotel, and she lay down on her bed and fell asleep immediately. She woke, an hour and a half later, soaked in sweat. Richard was reading a book. She went into the bathroom and showered, washing her hair and her whole body. When she stepped out of the bath, she felt wonderful. She splashed herself all over with Bellodgia cologne (her favorite scent; a week or two later Richard would tell her that he found it sickly). With a towel wrapped round her, she went back into the bedroom, to find Richard digging in the depths of his suitcase.

"I've got a present for you," he said.

"Oh, darling," she said. "How exciting!" It was quite bulky, in white wrapping paper. She undid it. It was a raincoat, shiny black, in a material like thin rubber, but with a very high gloss. It was lined, preposterously, with satin in a simulated leopard-skin pattern, black uneven patches on an orange ground.

"Goodness," she said, and repeated it, "my goodness," to give herself time to think. Something—no, everything—about the garment repelled her. What she eventually came out with was, "Is it going to rain? The weather looks so marvelous," she added, and then, feeling her response was inadequate, "but how sweet of you to think of it, Richard."

"Why don't you try it on?" he said.

"Now?" she asked, astonished.

"Yes, now," and he pulled the towel from round her and threw it on the floor. Then, standing in front of her, ignoring her body, he held the raincoat open, behind her, so that she could put her arms into the sleeves. It seemed so ridiculous, being helped, naked, into black shiny rubber and orange satin, on a hot afternoon in the South of France, that she gave a little nervous titter of laughter. "Oh, shut up, for heaven's sake. Just keep quiet," he said, pulling it tightly round her (she shivered at the slimy touch of the satin on her skin), doing up the four shiny buttons that went down the front, dragging the garment in at the waist, and fastening its buckle belt. Then he stood back, looking at her. "Shoes," he said, and he was over at the cupboard, picking up and dropping shoes, finally finding, seizing on, the pair of very high-heeled black shoes she had bought to please him ("I don't like always to be so much taller than you," he had said). Now he was kneeling in front of her, putting the shoes on her feet, and then he bowed right over and started to kiss her ankles. He glanced up. "My goodness," he said. His eyes were blank and hazed.

Then he was bowed down again, his forehead pressed against her ankles. Next he was nibbling and kissing up toward her knees. "Your slave," he murmured, kissing her thighs. His head was burrowing under the raincoat, his lips were on her pubic hair, and for the first time she herself felt sexually aware. But his hands were suddenly scrabbling with his belt, pulling it from the slots of his trousers, pressing it into her inert hand—in which he kept it by forcing her fist closed within his own. With the other hand he dragged at his white underpants, tugging them down. For the first time she saw his penis fully erect, as he wriggled forward and pressed it between her feet. And then he was clenching her fingers round the belt. "Now," he was moaning, "punish me now!"

She sprang back, violently disengaging her hand from his; dropping his belt to the floor; then tearing at the belt, at the buttons, of the raincoat; hurling it off behind her; kicking the shoes off her feet; he, reeling back, on his face an expression of total shock, which, as she exclaimed, "Vile, oh how disgusting, oh how vile," changed to one of pure loathing, of ungovernable rage. He staggered to his feet, half crouching, but at once moving toward her, his hands extended, to seize her—she knew it—by the throat. Turning, she rushed for the bathroom, was inside it, twisting the key in the lock, just before he hurled himself against the door. Once. Then silence. She sat down on the edge of the bath, trembling all over, staring at her face in the large mirror on the opposite wall, and then starting to cry—she didn't really feel like crying, but she couldn't think what else to do.

When she came out, cautiously, ten minutes later, Richard was gone, and so was the raincoat.

She never saw the raincoat again, but Richard returned that night—very late, and sounding very drunk.

Later she would be sure that that must have been when he started to hate her, but she never could have guessed it during the next ten days. For when—after stumbling into his bed in the early hours and falling at once into a heavy, snoring sleep—Richard woke next morning, he was all sweetness, all charm, just as he had been during their happiest times at university, making jokes, laughing, quite aglow with energy.

They lay on beaches; they swam; they drove, in their hired car, all along that overbuilt, but still astonishing, coast. Richard gambled in the casinos. She found their atmosphere oppressive, but she didn't really mind, because he seemed to enjoy it so much. They ate overlooking the harbor in Nice, and at *La Colombe d'Or*, just outside the walled village of St. Paul. Opposite the entrance to the restaurant's courtyard, men played *boule* on a dusty square of gound under a great tree.

Late one afternoon, they called (after visiting the Matisse museum—Richard all docile amiability) at the villa where Jessica's mother lived, in the Cimiez district of Nice. ("By all means, try your luck, darlings," Jessica had said when she gave them the address, "but don't be surprised at anything that happens.") However, the gray shutters on the windows of the faded-pink villa were closed. The only sound was the scraping of a cicada. A black cat, crouching on a stone wall, stared at them, then bounded down and disappeared behind some white-flowering oleanders. They could hear the bell pealing inside the house, but no one answered it, and Angie was glad to

retreat down the path between the thickly
growing shrubs and close the creaking gate behind
them. ("Probably in bed with a couple of sailors,"
was Jessica's only comment when they told her
about it on their return to London.)

The night before they left, Angie went to bed
early, exhausted after a day on the beach. Richard said he wasn't tired, and that he'd go for a
last walk round the town, and have a drink or two
in a café. She was woken—she didn't know what
time it was—by his turning her onto her back and
climbing on top of her. "You smell of perfume,"
she murmured, half asleep still. "Nonsense," he
said. Then he was inside her—a sudden sharp
pain—and a moment later he had come. *So that's
it,* she thought.

He probably "made love" to her, as she called
it, about twenty times in the next two years. Always it was the same: sudden, and over in a
minute. Then he would sigh deeply and fall
asleep.

But, looking back, she would decide that those
first two years hadn't really been so bad. For one
thing, she had been so busy.

First of all, there was doing up the house they
bought, at the back of Carlyle Square. Richard
would have preferred Eaton Square, but she got
her way on that. Belgravia depressed her, with its
great pillared houses, occupied by embassies and
by the very rich. Chelsea, she liked to feel, was
more mixed, more human, though that wasn't
true now in the way it must once have been.
Decoration was something else they didn't really
agree about, but here she surrendered, in regard
to most of the rooms, doing them up in the anonymous, rather grand manner he approved of. Only

in her own big studio-library, on the top floor, did she indulge her taste for rich colors, for oriental hangings, for divans and great embroidered cushions instead of chairs. At one end was a gallery of shelves for her books, behind her father's chair and desk (too heavy, really, for the room); and at the other end were her painting materials.

Here, increasingly, she retreated from Richard's friends—he and they were perfectly content that she should do so. She realized, without regret, that she bored them as much as they bored her.

They liked to gamble until the early morning or to sit around for hours in nightclubs; both were activities (inactivities?) which she detested. Whereas she preferred small, pretty restaurants, they patronized big grand ones with bowing *maîtres d'hôtel*. At weekends they migrated to the country, to kill birds and animals; she started evading those invitations very soon. But, on the whole, it could have been said that at this stage of their marriage, she and Richard led their own lives quite successfully. Twice a week she went to work in the Fulham studio of an illustrator of children's books—her drawing was steadily improving. She added to her book collection, and began to build up a very interesting cellar. When he saw that his friends regarded it with respect, Richard became quite proud of her taste in wine, though she always felt that at the same time, he thought there was something slightly freakish about it. Perhaps Cecily's pronouncement that "the man should always choose the wine" still lingered somewhere in his mind.

Cecily! How polite she and Angie were to each other, and how great was their mutual dislike. Cecily! With her little helpful hints about how to speak ("Not suit, Angie dear, coat and skirt; only men wear suits"), how to behave ("You simply must replan the seating; Freddie St. Law should be on your right"), even how to spend ("Don't you think that's rather an ostentatious tip"—this when Angie was taking her out to lunch). And a great many hints about how to look; for Angie was beginning to lapse in this regard. The little suits (coats and skirts) were being replaced by jeans and peasant clothes in the daytime, and she was starting to design romantic robes for the evening. "And, Angie dear, have you thought of trying a different hairdresser?" But Angie had given up going to the hairdresser altogether; she was letting her hair grow and straighten again. But though she felt that Cecily's hints were darts planted in her skin (how surprised Cecily would be if she suddenly whirled and charged at her like a little, maddened bull), she never let her feelings show. That was one thing she could do for Richard. He "adored" his mother—she supposed she should admire him for it. And indeed she did admire the delicacy with which he treated her. A generous allowance was deposited each quarter in Cecily's bank account, without his ever referring to it. Of course, the money was Angie's—but she was determined not to think about that. After all, when she married Richard, she had known that he was poor. That was, she now felt cynically, part of the bargain, though occasionally it crossed her mind to wonder what *her* share of the bargain actually amounted to. A handsome escort (though she seldom wanted to be escorted), a place in the world (a world which didn't interest her), a home of her own (though, of course, she could have had that anyway). But she was determined to make the best of things.

Loneliness? There was always Jessica. She would come in the afternoon, up to the studio, would sink down on a heap of cushions ("Mmm, darling, your delicious harem"), and chatter away just as she'd always done. Their relationship wasn't disturbed by her marriage (six months after Richard's and Angie's) to a pale-gold Old Etonian (an absurd way to classify anyone, really, but what other yardstick was there by which to measure Simon?). He had a curious resemblance to Richard; was, as it were, a pastel version of him—paler, slighter, far less animated. After a year the marriage ended. ("Mmm, the thing was, I found him rather sweet, rather touching, really. But one can't go on feeling touched indefinitely, can one? I ought to have chosen something rather *grittier*, I suppose. But the thing is"—a little sigh —"would that have been quite *me*?") A very amicable divorce—so amicable as to be scarcely apparent.

The only "thing was" that sometimes, nowadays, Jessica could be a little *sharp*. For instance, when Angie commented on Richard's "set": "Really, Angie darling, you're such a Puritan. It makes you *miss* things. There's something amusing about almost everyone. If one looks for it." Then she added, smiling again, "Aunt Jessica talks to the teens."

Angie found that she could never really discuss Richard with Jessica. One afternoon, soon after their honeymoon, she'd dropped a sort of hint. About how Antibes (that was how she put it) had been a little confusing. "Oh, well, darling, things are rather confusing sometimes. You know," Jessica had added, "all men have their little ways." And somehow she had sounded so final that Angie hadn't had the courage to say more.

That was the way things were, those first two years.

The sky clouded over; the weather was gray and showery. Angie started work on her stories the day after her visit to Fox Hall. However, she had no intention of driving herself too hard. She typed and sketched for three hours in the morning, and stopped at half past twelve, when she walked up to the Fox and Hounds. She sat there for an hour and a half, slowly drinking two half pints of lager, and reading a book. The old man was there in the corner each day, but the Donnisthorpes did not appear. Not on Wednesday, Thursday, or Friday. On Wednesday she was certain that they would be there. On Thursday she hoped. On Friday she decided that she would never see them again. Each day, back at the cottage, she ate a light lunch. In the afternoon she rested and read. Then she went for a drive. Going and returning, she always managed to pass Fox Hall, but she saw no sign of any of its inhabitants.

Each evening, she became a little drunk, sitting in the porch till twilight, then moving to her seat behind the kitchen table. When the darkness beyond the kitchen window became impenetrable, she would take her glass and a bottle and go upstairs to her bedroom, where she would draw the curtains (she didn't like the feeling of sitting in a lighted room with the world all dark outside). She wasn't afraid. Now she was sure that the stone head on the table had been a figment of her imagination. By ten o'clock each evening she was asleep, and she slept so well that she woke each morning feeling fresh and buoyant.

Saturday was radiantly fine again. The smell of warm damp earth and grass was all round her as she sat on the terrace, typing. The first of her fairy tales was nearly finished when she became aware that someone was knocking at the front door. She went round the side of the porch. Peregrine was standing by the door. The sight of him was a shock. She was glad she had a moment to adjust to it unobserved. He raised his hand to knock again. She said hello.

He turned. "Am I under observation?" he said. And that uncontrollable blush came up like a wave. She started to stammer out words about how nice it was to see him, and how was Vanessa and how was Woody.

He ignored these inquiries. "Thought I'd come and see how you were getting on. Are you feeling lonely yet?"

"Oh, no. Not at all," she said.

"Well then, perhaps I shouldn't disturb you."

"Oh, no . . . I mean, yes. It's lovely to see you. Come and have a drink."

"A most agreeable idea," he said, following her round the side of the house, past the horrible head in its bed. (She made herself look at it at least once a day; it was losing any terrors it had possessed for her.)

They were on the terrace. "Shall we sit down here? Do," she said. She picked up the typewriter and her papers, and carried them inside, and put them on the low table in the porch. She said to

Peregrine, "I won't be a moment," and went through to the kitchen, where she took out of the refrigerator a bottle of the 1953 Bernkasteler Doktor Feinste Auslese which she had put there after breakfast that morning. She placed the bottle and two glasses and the corkscrew on a tray, and took the tray out onto the terrace.

"I'll open that," he said, rising from the bench. He examined the label on the bottle. "Good heavens," he said, "I'm overwhelmed. Or do you usually drink this sort of thing?"

She laughed. "As a matter of fact, I do. My father always said that wine was something one shouldn't economize on."

"I must obviously visit you more often," Peregrine said, easing the cork from the bottle.

She lit a cigarette. "I know you don't smoke," she said, "but can't I get you something to eat? There are some Bath Olivers. Or wouldn't you like some nuts?"

He had poured the wine into the two glasses. He came toward her with one. "I don't want anything at all," he said, "except this splendid wine." He paused; he laughed. He said, "Well, certainly not anything to eat." To her intense annoyance, the blush returned. "Sit down, Angela," he said. "You're fluttering around like a butterfly." With his left forefinger he touched the base of her throat. "I shall have to fasten you down, like a butterfly, with a pin," he said, handing her the glass of wine.

They sat down, side by side, on the bench. "We thought," he said, "that you might like to spend the Saturday to Monday with us."

"The weekend?"

"Yes, at Foxers. We can sit in the garden. Or even in the conservatory, if the weather changes. And drink some wine. Though it won't be as splendid as yours. But perhaps you could put up with that?"

"Oh, yes," she said. "I'd love to come."

"Splendid," he said. "About six o'clock?"

That very smooth dark skin. The indentation of his nostrils. The thin curly line of his mouth. What was it? It was something more than the individual features. It was . . . *the idea of a mask* that his face brought to her mind. She wanted to touch it, to push at it with her fingers, to place, as children do, a finger at each corner of the mouth and tug it upward into a smile, or a finger above each eye—"Now you're Chinese!" She wanted, particularly, to run her fingers along his eyebrows, following the astonishing curve and then flicking in the bold little finishing strokes beneath the temples.

"Did your nanny never tell you it was rude to stare?" he now inquired, and burst out laughing.

"Oh, I'm sorry," she stammered. "I was miles away."

"Not really a very important rule anyway," he said. "Not nearly as important as 'Never ever let your gun pointed be at anyone.' "

They finished the bottle of wine. He refused the offer of a second. After seeing him to the door, she went back to the terrace. She looked at her watch. Half past twelve. In five and a half hours she would be on her way to Foxers. She waltzed a few steps. How happy she was. When had she last felt really happy, as opposed to not unhappy? When

was it that she'd started feeling unhappy most of
the time?

Of course, everything had been crumbling away,
decaying, eroding, without her noticing it, under
that superficial, oh so sensible calm in Carlyle
Square. It was when Richard gave up his job,
almost exactly two years after their marriage, that
the first great cracks began to show in the
facade.

He had stopped working for a week before she
found out. She'd called him at the office about
something, and the receptionist had said, "I'm
afraid Mr. Charteris is no longer with us." "No
longer with you? But that's nonsense." "Mr. Charteris left us last week," the receptionist said. "Is
there anyone else I can put you through to?" "Oh,
no thank you," Angie said, replacing the receiver.
When Richard came home that evening, at the
usual time, she waited for him to say something.
But after pouring himself a drink—she refused
one—he sat down and began to read the *Evening
Standard*. "You've given up work, I hear," she
said. He looked up from the paper. "What? Oh,
yes, I just couldn't stand it any longer. I'm looking
for something more interesting." He returned to
the "Londoner's Diary." "Oh, I see," she said.

But the weeks passed, and apparently nothing
more interesting turned up. Richard had recently
joined a club in St. James's—put up for it by one
of Cecily's old friends. Now he began to spend
most of the day there.

It wasn't that his salary made any difference to
the way they lived. It was the idea of his not
doing anything that she couldn't stand. "Puritan,"
she told herself, thinking of Jessica's words, but

she remembered her father, sitting at his desk hour after hour, with all those lists and columns, making his short decisive phone calls. One evening she said to him, "Richard, don't you think it's time you found another job?"

Later, at the dinner table—there were several people to dinner that night—Richard directed the first of his monologues at her. How familiar they were going to become in the months ahead.

It was her first tea party at university that was the subject that night. He made a meal of it, indeed, or rather a variety of meals.

"Cleopatra's boudoir, it was, except that poor Cleo hadn't a clue. I was meant to be the asp, but I just couldn't find her bosom. . . . I was Cinderella: I had to hurry away, because the room might have turned into a pumpkin at any moment. She just loves fairy stories, you know, my wife. . . . She was lurking in her lair like a black widow spider. I was terrified. Next time, I took Jessica with me, for protection. But, as you see, to no avail: she devoured me. But perhaps I'm slightly more difficult to digest than she imagined. These American women expect any man to dissolve at the first contact with their gastric juices. Perhaps because they haven't any others. Juices, I mean."

At the other end of the table Angie sat impassive in her green kaftan with its silver embroidery.

"There she sits, looking like something out of a second-class harem. Rather too shopworn for one of the better sultans, wouldn't you say?"

"Oh, now, come off it, Richard." One of the guests seemed to be enjoying himself less than the others—the younger son of some Scottish peer. Now he managed to change the subject. The words in Angie's mind were, *War has been declared*. What interested her was how little she cared.

But it wasn't quite as simple as that. Late that night, Richard was in her bed, apologizing. "Darling little Angie, forgive me. Can't really remember what I said, but I know I must have been awful. Terribly drunk. Titus, you know. Do you remember when you asked me what Titus meant?" This appeal to that past which he had been destroying so viciously a few hours before made her grit her teeth and clench her fists as he climbed on top of her. Thank goodness, it only took a minute, as usual. "You do forgive me, Angie?" he asked, rolling off her. "Oh, yes," she said. "I forgive you, Richard."

Did she? She didn't know. She didn't care. She wondered if this state of emotional anesthesia was permanent.

Life was easy for the next week or two. Daily, Richard measured out a brimming dose of his charm. Truce.

Till he met Kirsty Ewing.

She was lean and rangy, but with heavy breasts. Her pelvic bones protruded sharply from a tight black skirt or from trousers. She always wore black. Black turtleneck sweaters. Black boots. A black coat with epaulets. A black peaked cap. Black tights, with the curly black hairs on her legs pushing through the mesh. Her short hair framed her face in a spiky fringe, drawing attention to her big, strong, slightly yellow teeth and her glistening eyes like prunes soaked in brandy. She had a Scottish accent, a deep voice, and a harsh laugh with which she rounded off most sentences.

Angie couldn't bear Kirsty's being in the house, and suddenly she was there all the time. Sprawling on the sofa in the drawing room; dropping cigarette ash on the floor; lounging, her chair tipped back, at the dining-room table; covering everything she ate with a thick layer of tomato ketchup; steadily swilling down Scotch and Coca-Cola, with no visible results except that a dirty sort of chuckly undertone in her laugh came up more and more strongly.

Jessica detested Kirsty, too. "It's a pity they've stopped whipping whores at the cart's tail," she said to Angie. And then, with an unusual gentleness, "Don't worry, Angie. He'll get over it."

The way he looked at her—his eyes fixed on her, like those of an obsessive dog on its master, following every movement! Sometimes he would seem to forget where he was, just staring, with his mouth slack and a glazed look in his eyes.

With Kirsty came her hangers-on: a seedy journalist, a young man who did a drag act in a nightclub, an immensely fat blonde with tiny features buried in flesh and a little-girlish voice. They reminded Angie of cartoons of Berlin night life in the 1920s.

"I can't stand having that mob in my house," she said to Richard.

"*Your* house. How exquisitely tactful you always are, my dear Angie."

"I'm sorry. That's not what I meant. I just meant I don't like having them around. They give me the shivers."

"Well, they amuse *me*. And you can always retire to your refuge in the clouds, can't you? With your books and pictures and all the *finer* things."

She went out to a film. When she came back, she could hear their voices in the drawing room. Halfway up the stairs she met Kirsty, coming down from the bathroom. She stood aside for her to pass, but Kirsty stopped, and took Angie's chin in her hand. Kirsty stared into her face, and Angie stared back, hypnotized. Then Kirsty gave her laugh, and said, "Oh, I can see why *you* would never do for him. Yes, *I know you.*" And she went on down the stairs, leaving Angie astonished by an impulse to pursue her, to seize her by the arm and say, "Well, if you know, *tell me*. I want to know, too." But of course she didn't. Later she crept down to the basement, and fetched a bottle of Romanée-Conti, and fell asleep drinking it, in front of the fire in her studio.

She dreamed that Kirsty was pushing her in a swing. Her arms were twined like vines up the chains of the swing, and her wrists were fastened to the chains with handcuffs. "Higher! Higher!" Kirsty was shouting as she pushed her up toward the barnlike darkness of the roof. "Higher! Higher!" Kirsty was laughing, but Angie was screaming. She awoke. Feeling pleasure.

It was in the week that followed that Angie first went to bed with Joe, her drawing teacher, in his room in Fulham. She had always liked the room, which looked chaotic but was very clean. All his art paraphernalia was under the big north-facing window. In the middle of the room were a scrubbed-pine kitchen table and some Bentwood chairs. There was a big divan in an alcove, and a sink and a two-plate cooker were behind a Victorian nursery screen, pasted with scraps. Everywhere there were things to touch and to look at: a cracked *famille vert* plate, shells, a petrified branch, a wooden doll with bright red circles on its cheeks, a lump of quartz.

Joe had first reminded her of a mole because of a brown velour sweater he often wore. But there was also something molelike about his compactness and his very soft brown hair.

She had always recognized him to be attractive. Arriving or leaving, she had often passed beautiful girls on the stairs.

What she liked best about him were all the things that distinguished him so utterly from Richard and his friends: his classless accent, his untidy clothes, his ruffled, sleepy look. And, of course, his talent.

After her lesson that day, he said, as he often did, "Stay and have some coffee." It was getting dark. There was a fire in the grate, dimly lighting the room. He made the coffee in an earthenware jug, after grinding the beans in a hand grinder. She was sitting on the divan. He brought her her mug of coffee. She looked up at him, and he came down neatly on his haunches, put the mug carefully on the floor, and started to kiss her.

Little Angie and little Joe. They were two small, warm animals in a burrow. They were innocent. They rubbed noses. They licked each other's ears. They played. "Beatrix Potter lives," Angie murmured. Joe laughed. "The Flopsy Bunnies are very flopsy indeed," he said. He buried his face in her armpit and fell asleep.

"Hush," he had said to begin with, "hush. Calm down. You're like a little nervous horse. Relax. There's nothing in the world to worry about." For she had quivered and tensed, as was her body's

habit. And as now she did again—Joe asleep beside her—at a sudden memory of Richard's white
limbs.

All through that winter and the next spring,
there was Joe. She ran up the stairs and dropped
her black cloak on a chair, and the cloak slithered
to the ground. How safe it was, deep in the divan,
under the patterned Mexican blanket.

As her body blossomed, sometimes she felt a
curious kind of hunger. For something more.
What? She didn't know.

How she used to dread returning home. She
and Richard were hardly speaking these days,
except when he delivered one of his drunken monologues. He hadn't touched her for months—
thank God.

His infatuation for Kirsty was becoming more
and more blatant. Once, Angie came into the
drawing room and found her sitting in his lap,
tugging at his hair. Kirsty didn't move. "Oh, hullo, Angie," she said. Richard was gazing at Kirsty
with his drugged look.

It was soon after that Angie told him she
thought they should get a divorce. He looked astonished, then alarmed. "I can't see any need to
be so . . . extreme," he said. "We rub along pretty
well, most of the time, don't we? Perhaps I am a
little difficult occasionally, but not often. And
you're free to lead your own life." He looked at
her speculatively. "You've been going out a lot,
recently. Perhaps *I* should start checking up on
you."

The idea frightened her. She didn't want to get
Joe involved in anything sordid, so she didn't say
any more.

She was proud of how well she behaved when

Joe had to go to the States. An American publisher wanted him to illustrate a book, and had found him some part-time teaching at an expensive finishing school for girls.

"You should come with me," he said, but lightly, and when she exclaimed, "Oh, Joe, it's impossible," he didn't raise the subject again. She never talked to him about her marriage, and he never questioned her.

He was to leave on a Monday. She spent his last weekend with him. She told Richard she was going to drive into the country, and stay at some quiet hotel, and think things over. "Not still brooding on that mythical divorce, are you?" he asked. She shrugged her shoulders.

Saturday night. Joe had prepared a special, festive meal—*veal escalopes* in a wine sauce. He was an excellent cook. Before they ate, he lit two tall red candles. She had brought two bottles of the Roederer 1959 with her.

Late that night—the candles were guttering—lying in bed, she suddenly started to shake uncontrollably. "I feel so frightened," she said. "So terribly frightened." "But what are you frightened of, sweetie?" "I don't know. Being alone, perhaps. I'll be so terribly alone when you've gone." "Dear Angie," he said, "I shall miss you, too."

The next day was gray and heavy, and her mood was gray and heavy also. She felt quite numb with depression. She couldn't think. She couldn't talk. She drank a lot of Joe's terrible Spanish Chablis at lunch, hoping it would cheer her up. But it didn't. In the middle of the afternoon, she stood up. She said, "Joe, I must go." "But Angie, I thought you were staying till tomorrow morning," he said. "No, I must go now. I feel so terrible. I shall only depress you. And you'll be in such a rush in the morning. I'd only be in the way. I'll go home and take some aspirin and go to sleep." She managed to smile. "We didn't get much sleep last night."

Down the stairs. The familiar smell of the hall. For the last time. "Don't come down," she said, so he stood at the top of the stairs, leaning on the banister. "I'll phone you as soon as I get back," he said. "Yes. Yes, you must do that. Good-bye, Joe." Suddenly she wanted to rush back up the stairs. But she waved instead. "Good-bye," he called, and she was in the street, hurrying down it, past shabby gray houses, concentrating on getting to the car before . . . Before what? Before she broke down. But she didn't. She switched on the engine and drove home with the dull heavy ache in her head, in her chest. Drove home in the gray afternoon, toward the worst moment of her life.

Woody was sitting on the five-barred gate, in his vermilion T-shirt. As she approached, he jumped down and opened the gate for her to drive through. She pulled up on the other side, and he got in next to her.

"How nice of you," she said.

"Sir Peregrine's command. We provide *every* service at Fox Hall."

"What a marvelous evening," she said. A peach of an evening, swollen with ripeness, furred with a bloom of heat and stillness. Luscious.

The peacock pecked at the gravel. The stone of the house was gold in the early evening sunlight. Vanessa came across the cool dusk of the hall to meet her. "Come and see your room," she said.

Angie followed her up the stairs, carrying her

small overnight bag. She paused for a moment under the portrait of Peregrine's mother, and looked along the gallery. At the far end, on the right, was a grand piano. Vanessa turned left into a corridor. They passed several doors before she stopped at one and opened it.

"Oh," Angie said, "how romantic. I've never slept in a four-poster before."

The room was big and quiet. There was a fireplace with a carved mantelpiece. The walls were papered with a faded pattern of trellises and flowers. The bed had green hangings. Between the two long windows stood a bow-fronted chest of drawers. The only other furniture in the room was a Victorian cheval mirror with speckled glass, a small chintz-covered armchair, and a bedside table. On one wall was an engraving of a little girl holding a lamb. The door of a huge recessed closet stood open. Vanessa opened another door, which led into a bathroom containing a huge claw-footed bath, a hand basin, and a lavatory with a wooden seat. The basin and the lavatory were patterned with blue flowers.

"I'll leave you to wash and unpack," Vanessa said. "Come down when you're ready."

After Vanessa had gone, Angie couldn't help smiling at the idea that she would need to refresh herself after such a very brief journey. However, she unpacked her bag, arranged her cosmetics on the bow-fronted chest, and put her underwear in a drawer which was lined with yellowing paper and contained a sachet of lavender from which every trace of scent had faded. She hung the kaftan she had brought, in case they changed for dinner, in the big dark closet. She brushed her hair and put on a little pale lipstick. Then she went downstairs.

Peregrine was in the hall. "Angela, how lovely to see you," he said. "Come into the garden." They went through the conservatory. Beyond it was an overgrown lawn, surrounded by great bushes of old-fashioned white and pink roses. In the center of the lawn was a strange tree, tall, tyrannosaurus-shaped, its branches festooned with a brownish fringe.

"Weeping Wellingtonia," Peregrine said, seeing her looking at it. "*Sequoiadendron giganteum pendulum,* also known as the Mammoth Tree and the Great Tree of California. It's dead, of course. Struck by lightning ten years ago. But I can't bear to cut it down. Besides, I rather like it dead." There was a plaid rug on the grass, and three of the chairs from the conservatory were arranged round a white wrought-iron table. Woody came out of the conservatory with a tray on which were glasses and two bottles of Muscadet. Vanessa followed him.

Later, Peregrine fetched another bottle of wine. Dusk was falling, rooks had cawed and were silent, before they went into the dining room to eat cold chicken and gooseberry fool. Afterward, Woody brought coffee to the library. In a momentary silence Peregrine sprang to his feet. "Hide and seek," he said. "We shall play hide and seek. No arguments. I shall be he."

"But I don't know my way about," Angie protested. Beyond the library door, the hall stretched into shadow. "I'm not really very fond of the dark," she said.

"You must conquer these irrational emotions,"

Peregrine said. "Darkness," he added, "is merely the absence of light."

"I don't believe that," she said. "I think it has a life of its own."

"No arguments," Peregrine repeated. "Now, all scatter while I count to fifty." Obediently Vanessa and Woody stood up. Angie hesitated. Peregrine started to count: "One two three four ..." Vanessa and Woody were out the door. She couldn't stay behind. It would look so stupid. She got up. Peregrine was standing over by the window. "... eight nine ten eleven ..." She tiptoed into the hall. Where were Vanessa and Woody? They had vanished. She couldn't see or hear a sound of them. She glanced to the left, down the corridor to the conservatory; to the right, toward the dining room. "... twenty-three twenty-four twenty-five twenty-six ..." She panicked. In front of her was the staircase, and she ran up it. At the top, breathless, she looked to left and right. The grand piano loomed at the end of the gallery. She hurried to it, and crouched down behind it just as Peregrine shouted "Coming!" Then there was silence.

She could feel her heart thudding. She was panting a little. She crouched in the darkness, clinging to one of the piano's thick, turned legs. Still silence. Then she heard a step creak. Someone was coming up the stairs. Now he was singing, in a low voice,

> *A-hunting we will go,*
> *A-hunting we will go.*
> *We'll catch a fox, and put him in a box,*
> *And never let him go.*

Now she could see him at the top of the stairs, standing quite still, attentive. And then, reminding her suddenly of a robot, he turned to the right and started to move slowly toward her.

We'll catch a fox, and put him in a box,
And never let him go.

On the word "go" he suddenly launched himself forward, almost skidded toward her, swinging himself round the piano. She gave a little cry. And now he was crouching in front of her. He placed his hands on her arms, and gripped them for a moment. "*Got* you!" he said.

His face was just above hers. Surely he was going to kiss her. She yielded to an irresistible impulse, and closed her eyes. A long moment passed. Then, "Angela," he said. She opened her eyes. He was smiling. "We shall soon remove the velvet gloves," he said. He released her arms and stood up, extended a hand to help her to her feet as, from downstairs, first Vanessa, then Woody, called "Home!"

It was at lunch next day that Peregrine said, "We're going away the day after tomorrow."

"Away?" she said.

Woody intervened. "Away," he said. "On wings of song. Arrivederci Roma, and so on. They to Scotland where strange tweed-shrouded figures stalk the moors in stern pursuit of feathered chums. The glorious Twelfth! I for a wild wild week in sinful London."

"Yes, we shall be back in a week. Well, nine days," Peregrine said.

She had a hollow feeling in her stomach. "What

fun," she said brightly. And then—double bluff—"I shall miss you."

"You will be able to make progress with your book," Peregrine said. "I have a feeling that we have been providing too much distraction. I shall expect to see a mighty pile of manuscript on our return. We shall have a splendid celebration."

"Beaded bubbles winking at every possible brim," said Woody.

"Super," said Vanessa.

FOUR

The days passed slowly, but not unpleasantly. Monday was very hot, but on Tuesday there was a little storm. Wednesday was warm and gray. She drove into Bury St. Edmunds and renewed her supply of wine at an old-fashioned wine merchant's shop she found in a back street near the elegant little columned theater.

The days merged into one another. Each morning, sitting on the terrace or at the kitchen table, she typed on her portable typewriter, with its pretty, curly italic face. And she drew her fine spiky ink drawings: a princess awaiting her destiny, a little turreted castle, a nightingale singing its heart out in a dark wood.

The other thing she did was think about Peregrine. In the evenings, drinking her bottle of wine (she was very good that week; she never had more than one bottle), and afterward, lying in bed, she went over her recollections of him again and again. Two sentences of his, "I shall have to fasten you down, like a butterfly, with a pin" and "We shall soon remove the velvet gloves," she would repeat again and again, till they lost their meaning, but she knew that next day, their incantatory power would be replenished. "Coming," he called, and she crouched in the dark gallery till his figure appeared at the top of the staircase.

At the weekend the village changed; the people from London arrived. Station wagons were parked by the gates, and children played outside the cottages. On Sunday the Fox and Hounds was full of public relations men with scarves knotted round their necks, talking enthusiastically about village affairs, house conversions, and purchases from nursery gardens.

On Monday the village was itself again. There was no one in the pub at lunchtime, except the old man in the corner, and it was the same on Tuesday. Exactly a week since the Donnisthorpes had gone to Scotland.

She couldn't sleep that night. Eventually she went downstairs and opened a second bottle of wine and took it up to bed with her. After she'd drunk half of it, she fell into a doze. Everything in her head was thick, as if there were a stifling layer of cotton wool wrapped round her brain. She dreamed of a huge smooth snake which absorbed everything in its path: two small yellow chicks, a white rabbit . . . and then it was swaying over her. She sat up with a jerk. A little wind had risen while she slept. Downstairs a door banged and banged again, but she couldn't bring herself to go and find out where. She kept the light on all night, but she couldn't sleep again until after sunrise, although she finished the bottle of wine.

It was a gray, cloudy, stuffy day when she woke. She had a hangover. The thing to do, she knew, was to stick to her routine. But she felt a great weight of indifference dragging her down, keeping her in bed. She closed her eyes. "Peregrine," she murmured experimentally, but it didn't work. She tried to imagine him on a Scottish moor. Birds came over in a wave, and, like a machine, he fired, a bird dropping like a stone at every shot. She remembered the snake eating the chicks, and shivered.

She got up. She forced herself to take a bath, to make coffee, to put her typewriter on the table on the terrace. But she kept looking up sharply, as if something had flashed across the edge of her field of vision, or as if some strange sound were just on the brink of her awareness, scratching away beneath the normal garden noises. She left her current story abruptly, in mid-sentence. Every word sounded artificial. "And the Dragon said to the Princess . . ." She stood up. She'd take a break. Perhaps she'd go for a walk—down the lane that led beyond the cottage and out of the village. The lane dipped where there must once have been a ford; there were the remains of a crumbling bridge above the lane, and the ground was always damp. Did she want to go down into the dip in the lane where the dark trees arched overhead? *No!* Today she felt herself being dragged back into darkness, the ultimate darkness, the darkness that had descended so absolutely, after her discovery in the basement at Carlyle Square.

As she came to, she became aware of silence. The basement kitchen's normal gloom was intensified by the evening that was coming down outside. She was conscious of two pains: one where the back of her head had hit the floor, and the other on her chin, where, after he had grappled with her, he had struck her with the full force of his clenched fist.

Richard. *Where was he?* Slowly she sat up. Not a sign of him, not a sound. And then she became aware again of that great black plastic sack, and of the blood that was everywhere around. Like tomato ketchup, she thought, and in her mind a picture of the dirty plates and champagne bottles upstairs appeared and then was gone as she took in the reality of what surrounded her, here and now. She started to pull herself to her feet, clinging to the edge of the kitchen table. As her head came on a level with the surface, she saw the bloodstained kitchen cleaver that lay on top of it. That was when she tried to scream, and had that experience she had known in dreams, where her whole being was concentrated in the scream, and yet no sound came from her wide-open mouth except a hollow drawing-in of breath. Anyway, as she now told herself, screaming wouldn't help. Standing fully upright, she forced her eyes to travel over the whole surface of the room. The plastic sack leaned—bulging, sloping—against the kitchen cupboard. She took a step toward it in that descending dusk, and then moved fast—her foot skidded in a pool of blood—to the bottom of the stairs, where she pushed the light switch down. How much brighter the blood looked in the bright light! And then she was over by the sack. Her hand was on it when it lurched and fell toward her. She leaped backward. From the sagging mouth of the sack protruded the head of Kirsty, swollen purple, eyes staring, black, blood-soaked tights knotted tightly round the nearly severed neck. For one instant she just stood there, staring, and then she had turned, was scrabbling up the steps, was hurling herself along the passage to the front door—why wouldn't it open? Then it did, and she was out in the Sunday silence of the square, screaming now, screaming, "Help, oh help me!"

Somehow she had managed to grope her way through the next week or two. The questions, the policemen. Hiding from the reporters in a quiet hotel. For it was a sensation. Such a bloody murder was bound to be. And there was also the fact that Richard had vanished, had disappeared without trace. Day after day, in her hotel suite, she read the screaming headlines. CHELSEA BASE-MENT KILLER SIGHTED AT DOVER. But that, like so many that would follow, had been a false alarm.

He had strangled Kirsty upstairs, in his bedroom, where the police found a riding whip, cords and rubber garments, and a folder of pornographic photographs. Afterward he had dragged her body down to the basement. He had tried to make the body more manageable, but he had not proved adept with the cleaver, and had proceeded to force the mutilated corpse into the plastic sack. And that must have been when he had heard Angie coming into the house. A day earlier than he had expected.

The papers speculated about suicide. Angie didn't believe it. *Not Richard.* Why was she so sure of that? But she felt the police believed, as she did, that he was being harbored by some "old chum." Which one?

What had Richard's motive been? All that Angie could see was a picture of him in the hotel at

Antibes, crouching, moving toward her with his extended hands, that expression of wild fury on his face.

Jessica came to see her, curiously quiet and remote. "Poor Richard," were her first words.

"Poor *Richard?*" Angie repeated.

"Well, yes, of course." Jessica's gaze was cool; her tone was faintly surprised. And then, "Oh, my God, Angie, you don't mean to say you're feeling sorry for that frightful little whore. As far as I'm concerned, she deserved everything she got. She should," said Jessica the judge, "have known her business better."

"What can you mean?" Angie said.

"She should have known that you can't . . . let things go too far. Not when you're dealing with someone as unpredictable as poor Richard. People like that can . . . flip. Surely," Jessica said, "even if you didn't notice that personally, you could have learned it from your novel-reading."

There it had been, unmistakably, the contempt which she had found it so difficult to forget later, even when Jessica had proved so kind, such a tower of strength, her only friend. Jessica, she had tried to tell herself, was just . . . different. (*They* were so hard, she thought. It was as if they had drunk some steeling potion in their mothers' milk. Or, more probably, she reflected, in the bottled formulas that their nannies fed them.)

After Jessica's visit, a gathering darkness had deepened. But the visit from Richard's mother had been worse.

Wonderful, gallant Cecily, white as a sheet, cold as a stone, sitting opposite her in the hotel room, refusing tea, refusing a drink, saying, "He knew he couldn't turn to you."

Goaded, she said, "No, all he could do was turn *on* me." She fingered the fading bruise on her chin.

"Yes, because he couldn't trust you. He realized that *you'd* never help him. In spite of all that money."

Angie raised her eyebrows.

"Oh, I see what you're thinking now," Cecily went on. "And it is entirely typical of you. Just because I was prepared to let my son help me a little—and, after all, you could well afford it—you expect me to feel some kind of obligation toward you. Well, I don't. In fact, I blame you, blame you bitterly."

"Blame me? For what?"

Cecily's voice was low, intense. "For this whole thing. If you'd had any understanding of him, he would never have had to get involved with ... a woman of that kind."

"Do you really know what you're saying? What do you think I *am*?"

Cecily was standing up. "I think you're a nasty, spoilt, selfish little thing. Poor little rich girl, they say, don't they? Well, *I'm* not sorry for you."

Cecily was gone. So much blood, and so many questions. And now everybody hated her. Poor little Angie, she thought. Poor, poor little Angie. When the maid came in to turn down the bed, she found Angie sitting in a chair, muttering incoherently, unmoving, except for the fingers of her right hand, which plucked restlessly, ceaselessly, at the wool of her skirt.

She had to get out of the house. She looked at her watch. Half past eleven. Should she go up to the pub and have a drink? But the thought of the pub—with no hope of Peregrine, with just the old man sitting in the corner, nursing his pint of mild, and with Chullich pottering to and fro behind the bar—depressed her. She went to the store cupboard and took out a bottle of the claret she'd bought in Bury. She opened it and sat down at the kitchen table. Half an hour later, she heard a door bang in a gust of wind. She looked out of the window. A little spurt of rain dashed against the pane. She remembered that she'd left her typing on the terrace. As she went through the hall, the sitting-room door crashed again. (If one didn't close these old latches properly, the doors banged in the most exasperating way.) She went through the porch onto the terrace and picked up the typewriter. There were a few drops of rain on the page she had left in the machine. As she brushed them off, the last line caught her eye: "And the Dragon said to the Princess I'm going to put my prick in your cunt and fuck you dead." She stared at the words. There was another little gust of rain. Carrying the typewriter, she went inside the porch. She pulled the sheet of paper from the typewriter and read the line again. Then she put it down on the porch table, beside the typewriter, and went into the kitchen, where she poured herself another drink. She sat down on the bench behind the table.

She hadn't, couldn't have, typed those disgusting words. She was sure she remembered stopping work, leaving the words "And the Dragon said to the Princess"—the sentence unfinished. Yes, she was sure—or wasn't she? *The Unconscious.* She had a vision of a steaming, scummy pool. Had those words risen from her unconscious? Could

she have typed them without knowing it? Was
she, then, becoming ill again?

She had been in the nursing home for nearly a
year. She found it difficult to remember much
about the early part. Just the feeling of a thick fog
between her and the rest of the world, a fog
which Dr. Blaumann had gradually penetrated,
then gradually dispersed.

Had she done it to escape the case? She'd never
be quite sure. "You are a hysteric, not a schizo-
phrenic," Dr. Blaumann had said. Certainly, by
the time she had started to recover, the case had
started to fade from the press and from the public's consciousness. Rumors that Richard had been
sighted in France, in Australia, and, most recently, in Brazil, arose, but with decreasing frequen-
cy, as Jessica informed her. Jessica, who blew into
her private ward that spring, smelling of Diorissima, smiling, kissing her, saying, "Darling Angie,
I'm so so glad you're better. I've been longing to
see you, but I didn't know if you wanted to see
me. Rather foul, I feel I was, just after all that
drama. But you must remember I've known him
all my life. I couldn't help being a bit upset. Poor
old Richard." And this time Angie didn't mind,
even echoed, though rather doubtfully, "Yes, poor
Richard." It was so wonderful to be coming back
to life, and this coming back, she knew, involved
becoming reconciled to things. "But he's not
dead. I'm quite sure of that," Angie said. Jessica's
eyes were skeptical, her eyebrows raised. "Darling, do you really think? In some corner of a
foreign field? On someone's *hacienda*, with a lot
of cross old Nazis, drinking beer? Goodness, *that*
wouldn't suit Richard at all."

Anyway, the only thing that really mattered now was that Angie herself had been restored to life. She touched the leaves of the trees in the nursing-home garden and found them miraculous. She started to read again. She drank a split of champagne each morning at eleven. But there were so many things she had to do. Surprisingly soon, she started doing them. Just as she had after her mother's death. And so many of the things she had to do now were the same things she had done then.

She arranged for the house and its contents to be sold (except the books, except her father's desk and chair; she put them in store). She wrote letters about money. What was happening, she was informed, was that she was getting richer all the time. So that was all right! She wanted to initiate divorce proceedings but decided to wait a little longer, because she was afraid that a divorce case would start up the publicity again.

She moved into Brown's Hotel, but she didn't really like hotel life, and she knew she didn't really want to live in London. She had started, as a kind of therapy, to draw again, and her drawings told stories. That was how the idea of her book had been born.

And now, suddenly, into her book this obscenity had broken. She poured another drink. The stone head came into her mind. She saw it again, green-cheeked, in the pool of light. Lying on this very table at which she was sitting now. How had she been able to evade the horror of that so easily? She knew the answer. The day after, she had met Peregrine, and had become obsessed. And now that he wasn't there, she was going back into herself, was possibly starting to break down. She mustn't let it happen. Suddenly she longed to talk to someone. How she wished she had a telephone. But, of course, she could use the one outside the pub. That was it. She'd go up to the Fox and Hounds and get a lot of change from Chullich, and then she'd ring Jessica from the call box. She might even suggest that Jessica come down for a day or two. That bracing, skeptical presence would be sure to do her good. Jessica would be certain to find some practical explanation for everything. "Darling, it's just that you've been getting too pissed. You must start cutting down on the booze." That was the sort of thing Jessica would say. Might there be some truth in it? Yes, it would be wonderful to see Jessica. Except—what? She realized that she wasn't eager for Peregrine and Jessica to meet. Fascinating Jessica! She went round the cottage, closing the doors and windows, before walking up to the Fox and Hounds.

She fetched her half pint of lager from the bar. The old man was in his corner. While she was having her drink, a couple of young people on bicycles arrived. A boy and a girl. Sunburned and healthy, wearing shorts, giggling and holding hands under the table. Certainly not members of the upper class.

Chullich produced the coins for the telephone. The call box was very clean and tidy, with untorn telephone directories and no graffiti—very different from a London one. On a childish impulse she looked up the Donnisthorpes' number in the local directory. There it was: Donnisthorpe, Sir P, Fox Hall, Clave. Absurdly, she dialed the number and listened to the phone ringing in the empty house.

After a minute she clicked down the receiver and dialed Jessica's number. The phone rang and rang, unanswered. Jessica must be out. She would try again later, she decided, setting off down the hill, back to the cottage.

Telephoning Jessica became an obsession with her that afternoon. Particularly after she had finished the second bottle of wine and started on the third. Up the hill she trudged; she knew she mustn't drink and drive, and anyway, she'd look ridiculous driving up and down, up and down. If anyone were watching. She wondered why one saw so few people in Clave. Of course, many of the cottages belonged to weekenders. But there must be some local people. She supposed the men were out at work all day, and the women were busy with all those things country women were meant to be busy with: preserving fruit and vegetables, for instance; but, presumably, they couldn't spend *all* their time doing that. Baking bread and heating up the kettle for the laundry, perhaps. She smiled. Her ideas were hopelessly out of date.

On her fifth trip to the call box, after Jessica's phone had rung and rung, she decided she must take some other form of action. She tried to remember the names of other friends of Jessica's. But at that moment she couldn't think of anyone. Except, of course, her own former mother-in-law. Not quite former yet. (Soon she must really do something about that divorce.) Anyway, she knew Jessica kept in touch with Cecily. "I can't see why," Angie had said. "She's had a bad time," Jessica answered, "losing Richard. After bringing him up all on her own." "And a very bad job she made of it," Angie said. Jessica laughed briefly.

"You know, Angie, I find it very odd that you reserve your astringency for poor old Cecily. I can think of much more suitable objects." All the same, Angie had continued to pay Cecily's allowance. Secretly, it gave her a kind of pleasure to be so magnanimous to that horrid old witch.

So, why shouldn't she telephone Cecily to see if she knew where Jessica was? Because the idea rather appealed to her, she knew she must be pretty drunk. She remembered the number and dialed it. The phone rang only twice before Cecily answered it: "Hullo?"

"Oh, hello," Angie said. "It's me. Angie. I wondered if you could tell me where I can get hold of Jessica."

"Jessica?" Cecily said.

"Yes. I've been ringing and ringing her number without getting any answer, and I wondered if you might know where she was."

"But she's abroad," Cecily said. "Didn't she tell you?" Cecily sounded delighted that Jessica hadn't.

"Abroad?" Angie said. "Abroad where?"

"Oh, it was the most enchanting opportunity. Some old friends. They have an island. In the Caribbean somewhere. And they thought poor Jessica was looking tired. So they asked her to come and stay for as long as she wanted. Flight paid and everything. Dear Jessica—she has such a wonderful gift for getting on with people."

Unlike guess who, you mean, Angie thought. She said, "So you don't know when she'll be back?"

"I haven't the remotest idea, I'm afraid. I'm *so* sorry."

Like hell you are, she thought, but what she

heard herself saying was, "And what have you heard from Richard lately?"

There was a second's pause, then, "Vulgar, cruel, *stupid* girl," Cecily said, and rang off.

Angie stood for a moment, still holding the receiver to her ear. It suddenly felt very airless in the call box, and she replaced the receiver and pushed open the door. She stood outside, on the grass verge. Her heart was beating very fast, and she had a sense of being deserted. Of being absolutely alone. Jessica could have let her know. Why hadn't she? She remembered Jessica's profound aversion to writing letters: "I adore chatting away like mad for hours and hours on the telephone, but put a pen in my hand, and dot dot dot, the rest is silence." All the same, she could at least have sent a postcard. Perhaps she had. Perhaps the postwoman, in her blue uniform, would march up the path with it tomorrow. However, that thought did nothing to abate the sense of isolation she felt now. And she was also conscious of feeling ashamed. That last remark she had made to Cecily had been inexcusable. If she hadn't been so needled, she would never have made it. And did she really believe that Cecily knew where Richard was? She *could* probably have fixed his escape through some of those devoted important friends of hers. But *would* she? Didn't she have too profound a respect for Law and Order? Dear sweet Cecily had always been demanding the return of hanging, and longer prison sentences, and the birching of delinquent boys. But wasn't all that, when it came to the crunch, really meant for *Them,* as opposed to *Us?* Particularly as Richard had happened to dispose of a singularly undesirable representative of *Them*. One so hideously successful, and at *Our* expense. Showered with *Our* money and with so many of *Our* men kneeling pleadingly at her feet for fear or favors. Anyway, apart from all that, Angie was sorry about what she'd said to Cecily. Ought she to ring her again and apologize? She detested the idea, but after a moment she went back into the call box. Cecily's number was engaged. A sign from the gods, Angie decided, her mood lightening, and she set off along the road.

But, halfway down the hill, she turned back. She had suddenly decided that she'd ring Dr. Blaumann. She'd tell him there were one or two things she'd like to talk to him about. Perhaps she'd make an appointment to see him. She couldn't help feeling that just to hear that calm, deliberate voice would reassure her.

His receptionist answered the phone. "Could I speak to Dr. Blaumann?" "I'm afraid that Dr. Blaumann is away on holiday for the next two weeks. Can I help you at all?" "No. No, it's all right," Angie said, and she put down the receiver.

It wasn't her day for making phone calls, she decided. First, the disappearance of Jessica; then, dreadful Cecily; and now, the absence of Dr. Blaumann. She would just have to manage on her own. She must look upon it as a test. A test of her ability to survive. She mustn't let herself down. That was the way to think about it.

As she passed the church, an impulse possessed her: to visit the kingdom of the Donnisthorpes again. She went round to the front of the church and up the little path. She turned the iron handle and went inside, and up the aisle between carved pews.

She stood in front of the monument to the tenth baronet. His strange turbaned headdress could not disguise his astonishing likeness to Peregrine. She cast a furtive glance down the shadowy aisle. Then, on tiptoe, she leaned forward. She pressed her lips against those of the statue, but at once drew back. The chill of the marble, colder than ice, had seemed to strike down to her heart.

She found her feet dragging as she approached the cottage. There was something about its smug windows, its cozy flower beds, the roses on the wall, that seemed false to her. "A misrepresentation," she murmured, but could not clarify the thought.

Once inside—she hummed a tune loudly as she let herself in—she knew that she must go and look again at that sheet of paper, at those words. She went to the porch. The paper lay where she had left it, next to the typewriter. She picked it up. "And the Dragon said to the Princess"—but the other words were gone.

After that, the only thing that occurred to her was to drink herself to sleep.

She woke early next morning. Light was slowly seeping into the room. She looked at her watch. The time was just before five. She huddled down in bed, pulling the sheet tight under her chin, screwing her eyes shut, gathering herself into such a clenched fetal position that she felt like a snail. How she wished she had a shell to protect her. Sleep must return, to loosen the stretched feeling of the skin of her forehead, to dull the rhythmic throb somewhere at the back of her head, to relieve the dryness in her throat. Sleep must return, but it refused to.

She lay like that for a long time, trying to empty her head of the words that had appeared and then vanished, of the stone head in the pool of light, but the images persisted, rising again and again, sharply, from the cloudiness of her mind. She tried to think of Peregrine ("We shall soon remove the velvet gloves"), but the words sounded sinister instead of exciting. She was suddenly consumed by a terrible restlessness. She turned over. Then, after a moment, she got up and went through to the bathroom for a glass of water. It didn't help the dryness in her mouth. It seemed to be absorbed without effect—and what a dead chemical taste it had. She started on a second glass, but it made her feel nauseated, and she went back to the bedroom and lay down on top of the patchwork cover, which she had been too drunk to take off and fold, in her usual way, the night before. (Her clothes were scattered round the room. Well, at least she hadn't slept in them.) Though her mind was dull, it seemed to be twitching with the kind of reflex which she'd heard—thank heaven she'd never seen it—kept a chicken running after its head had been chopped off.

She felt reluctant to go downstairs to confront the mess of empty bottles in the kitchen, to face the earthy smell which was at its most intense in the morning because the windows had been closed all night. All the same, she got up. She took a long hot bath, which made her feel a little better, but not much. She put on clean clothes and, leaving the tousled bed unmade, went down the stairs slowly and reluctantly, clinging to the wall, feeling that she might trip on each steep tread.

The earth smell was there, and something more. It was as if a layer of depression, of doom (but that was an exaggerated word), lay like thick dust on the surface of everything. Odd that she hadn't really felt mad yesterday, in spite of the hallucinations, but today, in this grayness, with the birds' songs sounding like tape recordings instead of spontaneous effusions of joy (were birds glad?), she felt, each minute, that her mind might crack open.

She forced herself to go round the house, opening the windows and doors. She gathered up yesterday's five bottles (Five!—but she couldn't bear to think about *that* now) and stuffed them into the dustbin. Somehow she had used six glasses; she didn't feel like washing them. She sat down at the kitchen table, but got up again after a moment and went to stand in the front doorway. The day was heavy; there had been too little rain to clear the air. She went down the garden path to the gateway. In the village no one was stirring. Thursday. Tomorrow evening the commuters would arrive. On Saturday the men would be working in their gardens, and the women would be "homemaking," just the way they did in town. She'd seen one, with a scarf tied over her head, emptying what must presumably be the second Hoover (one for country, one for London) into the dustbin. Their dustbins would certainly not be full of bottles: she'd seen the men, in the pub the previous Sunday, exchanging one or two empty beer bottles for full ones. Their wives stayed at home, cooking the Sunday joints which she had smelled roasting in the cottages as she walked through the village. And then, on Sunday evening, they'd pack up and return to London. *What was the point*? That was one thing she'd never understood: the point of that kind of life. Perhaps that was why she'd fallen for two such unbourgeois men. Richard and Peregrine. She hated their arrogance but didn't she prefer it to the nothingness of the commuters? Though this morning, standing in the gateway, looking at the deserted village, she suddenly felt that she wouldn't have minded seeing a couple unloading trays of seedlings from the back of a station wagon, a small child pushing a doll's pram along the grass verge, a boy in shirt and jeans, trying to ride a bicycle without using his hands.

She felt something move on her left, in the garden of the Tudor cottage next door. She turned her head sharply and saw nothing, but the sudden jerk of her head brought tiny little specks before her eyes. She really must do something. But what? She didn't like the thought of being closed in the car, or of going through the motions necessary to propel it along the road. Nor did she like the idea of going back into the cottage, though at least it would be aired a little now.

She should concentrate on something, do some work. But the thought of the typewriter, of the unfinished sentence, or of the alternative of drawing a fine pen line with the hand which she now held up, shaking, in front of her face sent her mind off into a flight of panic. She went through the gateway and started walking away from the cottage, to the left, along the grass verge. How dense the thicket of the next-door garden was. Almost as dense as the trees at Fox Hall, but the growth was lower and bushier. She reached the little white gate of the Tudor cottage. The cottage looked quite well kept, though the garden was so dense and wild, but she'd never seen anyone going in or coming out.

She looked up the path. It really was a fairy-tale place. Why shouldn't she go and have a look round? She suddenly remembered the witch's cottage in *Hänsel and Gretel,* and hesitated. But that was absurd. She glanced behind her. In the village nothing stirred. She opened the little white gate. It creaked loudly, and she hesitated again. *Don't be a coward,* she told herself, and started up the path. The cottage was so tiny. The two little leaded windows under the thatch looked like eyes. There was only one window on the ground floor. She decided she'd look in and see if the place was furnished or not. But just before she reached the window, a hand came up from below it, inside, and twitched a curtain right across it.

She turned and ran down the path. She pushed the gate open. She heard it creak behind her and turned, once, to see the curtained window. Then, on she stumbled, along the grass verge and through her own gateway, up the path, through the front door—slamming it behind her—and through to the kitchen, where she slumped down at the table, gasping for breath.

Really, she told herself as she recovered, she had behaved ridiculously. Why had she been so horrified? Probably the cottage was occupied by some hermit, some old man or woman who feared the outside world, and who, hearing her approach, had panicked. But why had the hand come from *below* the window? She could see it now, clawing up like a crab.

She became conscious of her head again. It was throbbing dully. She looked at her watch. Only ten o'clock. A whole day to get through before she could sleep, in order to wake next morning feeling better, "feeling herself again," as people said. But what was "herself"? She was beginning to feel less and less sure. This whole venture had probably been a mistake. Dr. Blaumann had been right when he suggested, so tactfully, that she might not be ready for it. So what was holding her back from admitting it had been a mistake? Jessica's opinion? That was absurd. Jessica, when she returned from wherever she was, could say what she liked. And what, after all, gave Jessica the right to criticize her? (She would have to take up a bolder stance in *that* relationship.) What was it, then, that was keeping her here? The answer was simple. It was one word: "Peregrine." That was probably foolish, too. Mightn't she be dreaming her life away? ("When fantasy becomes dominant, it is destructive rather than creative," Dr. Blaumann had said.) After all, Peregrine had never really said anything concrete. Anything she could take hold of. Wouldn't the very best thing she could do be to pack up and leave before the Donnisthorpes returned? To decide not to play games any more. After all, there was Vanessa, who had been kind to her. She had nothing against Vanessa. How would Vanessa feel if anything developed between her and Peregrine? In fact, she should get into the car, now, and drive to London. She could hire someone to pack and fetch her things. Or, if she didn't feel like driving—which she didn't—she could go up to the call box and ring for some local taxi to take her. That was a better idea. So shouldn't she do that?

We shall soon remove the velvet gloves. And she saw herself going round and round in the ballroom, held by that hand on the base of her spine. *I shall have to fasten you down, like a butterfly, with a pin.* She had to stay.

He would be back tomorrow. She had to find out how things really were. Why shouldn't she? She had been starved for so long. Why shouldn't she be hungry for Peregrine? Wasn't he hungry for her? *We shall soon remove the velvet gloves.* He must be. She would stay.

The morning passed easily, once, at eleven o'clock—not a moment earlier—she opened one of the two remaining bottles of claret from Bury. After all, why shouldn't she have a drink? It would make the time pass more quickly, and she had admitted to herself that her immediate object was to pass time. And it would blur the outlines of all those things she didn't want to remember. The head on the table—not *that* again. The words on the paper—she had been drunk. The crab-hand coming up—why should she worry about that? All the same, she didn't want to go out onto the terrace, with its view of the thicket of that cottage garden. In winter, she wondered suddenly, would a thin trail of smoke from its chimney hover above the bushes?

When she opened the second bottle at half past one, she knew that she must have something to eat. She opened the store cupboard and peered around inside. Her eyes lighted on a packet of spaghetti, and she suddenly felt ravenously hungry. A big plate of spaghetti. Not Bolognese, not Napolitana. Just with butter and cheese and salt and a great deal of freshly ground black pepper. She had all the ingredients. With a sense of satisfaction she put a saucepan of water on the stove to boil. She hadn't been cooking enough proper food. Steak, people would tell her. A red slab of meat. No one ever seemed to eat anything else in the States, and now, in Europe they were crazy about it, too. She'd always despised people who ordered boring old steak in restaurants.

By the time she had cooked nearly half the packet of spaghetti, eaten it—she really had been hungry—and finished the second bottle of wine she felt amazingly relaxed and satiated. She gave a huge yawn, and realized with a sense of joyous wonder that she would be able to fall asleep. She did all the washing up—she really felt *much* better—and then climbed the stairs. In her room, still wearing her clothes, she crawled into the tousled bed, and huddled down.

It was dark. She knew that some sound had woken her. What had it been? She stretched out her arm and fumbled hastily for the bedside light. Her hand found the switch, and pressed it. Nothing happened. She sat up, clutching at the bed-clothes. Then she leaped out of bed and over to the door, next to which was the switch for the light in the center of the ceiling. She pressed it down, but the darkness remained unbroken. And then she heard the sound which she knew had woken her. Someone was laughing. It started very low—a chuckle—and then ascended a mad, ir-regular scale. Up at the top—how high it went!—it paused, and then descended. In the silence that followed she was frozen. Where had it come from? It had sounded as if it were in the bedroom on the other side of the large cupboard space. The laugh was repeated, and she was sure. Then she became aware of another sound, coming from the window. Something was scratching at the glass.

What could it be—up here, so many feet above the ground? From the room beyond the cupboard the hideous laugh repeated its upward and then downward journey.

Her hand was on the latch of the door. She was out, through the bathroom, stumbling, scrambling down the stairs, willing herself to be blind, deaf, her shoulders cringing from the expected clutch of a hand.

But no hand materialized. Downstairs the light was on. In the center of the hall stood the black plastic sack, lumpy, swollen. Red seeped from the top of it, down its side. "No," she moaned, shrinking against the staircase, "oh, no."

From outside, five notes sounded. For a second her mind couldn't take them in. . . . *D'ye ken John Peel*. . . . And then . . . she was past the bag; she was opening the front door; she was running down the path, calling his name. "Peregrine, Peregrine!" The Rolls was by the gate, and he was jumping out of it.

"Angie!" His voice was astonished. "What's the matter? Did I frighten you, blowing my horn?"

Speechless, she shook her head, pointed toward the house. But he was opening the back door of the car, gently pushing her inside, getting in after her.

"Now, hush," he was saying. "Be still. Be calm. Don't say anything until you've pulled yourself together." He put his right arm round her, patting her shoulder. He took both her hands in his left hand.

"The sack, the blood," she said.

But, "Hush," he said again. "You're not to say a word until you're calmer." Now, with his right hand, he stroked her hair. She rested her head against his chest.

Gradually—so safely held there—she shivered less, her breathing slowed. She became aware of the silence of the night. Somewhere in the distance a car started. His hand still stroked her hair.

"Well," he said. "Do you think you can talk now?"

"Inside," she said. "In the hall. A sack. All bleeding."

"What can you mean? I must certainly investigate. We'll go together and see."

"No," she moaned, "no."

"Come on," he said. "We'll go and face it together. You know you don't have to be afraid with me. Do you?"

Gently he detached himself, took his arm from round her, released her hands. He opened the car door and got out.

"Come on," he beckoned, and she stumbled out after him.

Her knees felt as if they were going to give way. "I can hardly stand," she said. "I'm shaking so."

"Then I shall have to carry you." He smiled. How calm he was. He lifted her up. "Light as a feather," he said, and with her head on his shoulder, her legs dangling over his arm, he carried her up the path to where light streamed from the open front door.

As he crossed the threshold, she buried her face in his shoulder. "I can't look," she murmured. He took a step or two, then paused.

"Angie," he said. "Open your eyes. Come on, now. Be a brave girl."

So, with all her will, she forced herself to turn her head, to open her eyes. Under the light the floor was bare. The earth smell rose to her nostrils.

"I can't believe it," she said. "It was here, under the light. The sack. And upstairs there was the laugh, and the scratching noise. The lights wouldn't go on."

Gently he deposited her on her feet. "I'll go and see," he said. "You stay here." He laughed. "Light as you are, I can't carry you up those stairs."

"Don't leave me," she said, but he took her by the hand, led her to the staircase, and lightly pressed her shoulder till she sat down on the bottom step. He bounded up past her. She could hear him pressing a light switch, opening doors, striding through the rooms. Her blank gaze circled the empty hall.

He was down again. "No one," he said. "The lights all switch on. There's nothing there."

She started to moan. "Now, Angie, control yourself," he said firmly. Again he lifted her up. He carried her over to the front door. He switched off the light. "We'll fetch anything you need, tomorrow," he said. "But tonight the important thing is to get you away from here."

He slammed the door behind them. He carried her down the path. "You're coming home with me," he said. "Home to Foxers. Safe and sound."

PART II

FOX HALL

ONE

Sunlight was flooding into the room through the long windows. She stretched out her hand and switched off the bedside lamp, the base of which was a cracked blue and white Chinese jar. Birds were twittering in the garden. The peacock gave one of its harsh cries.

She looked at her watch. The time was nearly eleven. How late she'd slept. But it had been three o'clock before she had crawled between the sheets —white linen, like her own, but fine with age, the monogrammed *D* on hem and pillowcase almost worn away.

How sweet they'd been to her! As Peregrine drove onto the gravel, he had sounded the horn. The five notes blared out loudly in the night silence. A moment later, Woody flung open the front door. Light streamed onto the gravel. Then Woody was by the car, opening the door for her. Slowly she slid her feet out, and stood up. The warm breeze brushed her cheek. Peregrine came round beside her, and put a hand under her elbow. "Can you walk," he asked, "or must I get into the habit of carrying you everywhere?"

She smiled. She shook her head. "No, I can walk," she said.

Vanessa was in the hall. "Why, what's the matter? How pale you look!" she exclaimed to Angie.

"She was frightened," Peregrine said. "All alone in that gloomy cottage."

"So you brought her here. Super!" Slightly awkwardly, Vanessa patted Angie's shoulder. "Peregrine was determined to go and find out how you were as soon as we got back," she said. "How lucky!"

"A damsel in distress," declared Woody. "Rescued by the gallant knight on his charger!"

"Do be quiet, both of you," Peregrine said. "The poor girl doesn't know whether she's coming or going."

They moved into the library. "Sit down," Peregrine told her. She sank onto the sofa. "Brandy," he pronounced, going over to the drinks tray. "I know you don't usually drink spirits," he said, "but this is an exceptional occasion. And after the brandy, some tea, I think. Woody, go and make some tea, will you? And what about something to eat, Angela? Or have you eaten?"

She had to make an effort to remember. Then, "Oh, yes," she said. "Lots and lots of spaghetti. And I'm not at all hungry. I couldn't eat a thing."

"Very well," Peregrine said. "Just tea then, Woody." Woody departed, and Peregrine brought her a glass half full of brandy. She took a sip. Then she rested her head against the back of the sofa, and closed her eyes. But behind her lids, the bulging black plastic, the oozing red stain, appeared. She opened her eyes, and sat up abruptly.

Later, drinking cup after cup of the hot strong Darjeeling tea (she'd never much liked tea, but tonight it was exactly what she wanted), she told them everything. Not just the things that had happened at the cottage, but also what had happened in the past, and who she was. ("The Charteris case. I say!" Vanessa exclaimed, eyes popping. But at least, Angie reflected, for once she didn't add "Super!") She told them about her breakdown and its cure. "But now," she said, trying to smile, "I seem to be madder than ever. I've never *seen* things before."

"Ah," Woody interjected, "wait till it's green rats and pink elephants. That's when you have to worry. I," he said rather proudly, "actually saw a green rat in *my* time of trial and tribulation."

"Angela isn't suffering from delirium tremens, Woody," Peregrine said coldly.

"Though I have to admit," Angie said thoughtfully, after a moment, "that I have been drinking rather a lot lately."

"You've been under a great strain, my dear girl," Peregrine said. "I'm quite sure it was the wrong thing for you to be all on your own in that dreary little hovel. You need company. You shouldn't have the opportunity to sit about and brood."

"You're probably right," Angie said. "My doctor was doubtful about it, too. I don't know what he'll say when I tell him about stone heads and obscene messages ... and sacks!" She shivered uncontrollably.

"*Do* tell us what the obscene message was,"

Woody broke in mischievously. "I'm positively *devoured* with curiosity."

"Oh, no. I couldn't possibly." She shook her head.

"You're embarrassing Angela, Woody," Peregrine said reprovingly. "She is a girl of very delicate sensibilities."

"Ever so Jane Austen, I'm sure," Woody said, rather caustically.

"Though I suppose," Angie said, pursuing her own train of thought, "that if the message wasn't there, I must have invented it myself. Unconsciously."

"All this psychology stuff is quite beyond me, I'm afraid," Vanessa said, with a touch of aggression. But then she grinned—the teeth again—apologetically.

"I must get back to London tomorrow," Angie said. "My own doctor's away, but I'll have to see another one. Dr. Blaumann's got a partner," she went on. "I could probably talk to him."

"Oh, but why rush off?" Peregrine said. "I'm sure that tomorrow you'll be far too tired to move. Personally, I'm convinced that my prescription is the right one. Rest, and people to talk to, and three square meals a day. Why don't you stay on with us for a bit?"

"It would be super to have you," Vanessa chimed in, nodding emphatically.

"Foxers, the famous health farm," Woody said.

"Oh, no. I must get back," Angie repeated. "I'm sure I should see a doctor right away."

"Well, we'll talk about it tomorrow," Peregrine said. "But now I'm quite sure that Angela should go to bed." He smiled at her. "A good night's sleep will work wonders."

"If I can sleep," she said, thinking of the black plastic, the crimson blood.

"I've got some amazing pills," Woody announced. He sprang to his feet. "I'll go and fetch them," he said. "Two of those and you won't know a thing till morning."

He had been quite right, she confirmed now, stretching in the bright daylight. Minutes after getting into bed, leaving the bedside lamp on, she'd been asleep. Could last night at the cottage really have happened? she wondered. The sun shone. The birds exchanged their messages. And she felt so well. How could she have had those hallucinations last night, and now be feeling so sane, so calm, so safe? Anyway, back in London, when she saw the doctor, she'd sort everything out. She heard a gentle tap on the door. "Come in," she said, sitting up in bed.

Vanessa peered round the door. "Did you sleep well?" she asked. She came farther into the room. "How are you this morning?" she inquired.

"Oh, so much better," Angie said. "I slept wonderfully. Woody's pills certainly are effective."

"Super," Vanessa said. "I wondered if you'd like some breakfast brought up?"

"Oh, no," Angie said. "I'll get up now. It looks like a lovely day. I'll be down in a few minutes. I'll just take a bath. I'm sorry I've only got dirty clothes to wear," she added.

"Oh, but Woody has fetched your suitcase from the cottage," Vanessa said. "He packed up everything he could find. We thought you'd need some of your things."

"You're all so kind," Angie said.

Later, at lunch, she said to Woody, "Do you think we could drive over to Clave, and fetch my car?" She didn't want to go anywhere near the cottage, but she felt that she ought to face it. "I really should get off to London quite early this afternoon," she said.

"Angela, you are not traveling to London today," Peregrine pronounced. "In fact, I absolutely forbid it. Tomorrow, possibly. Provided that you don't still look so pale."

"Oh, do stay and keep Peregrine company this evening," Vanessa said. "I have to go to a ghastly committee meeting, a Women's Institute thing, on the other side of Cambridge. And Woody is going to drive me. There's some old film in Cambridge he wants to see."

"Bette Davis, my dear, in *Dark Victory*, at the Film Society," Woody said. "She goes blind, and plants some bulbs, and then goes upstairs and *dies*. I shall cry my tiny eyes out."

"Angela, please don't desert me." Peregrine directed the full blaze of his charm at her. "Surely you can't resist such a desperate appeal?" he added, smiling.

She couldn't. "All right. Tomorrow it shall be, then," she agreed.

"After all, tomorrow, as Scarlett O'Hara remarked, is another day," said Woody.

She followed Woody and Vanessa into the kitchen at half after six, and sat and chatted to them as they ate poached eggs on toast and drank tea at the big pine kitchen table, which was white with age and scrubbing. The room was large and high-ceilinged. Along one wall extended a black iron range on which stood a giant kettle. A small yellowed 1930ish refrigerator was opposite it. The porcelain sink had a wooden draining board. In one corner of the room, an old armchair was drawn up in front of a small television set.

"This is where I sneak away to watch the midnight movie," Woody said. "Peregrine won't allow such a vulgar modern gadget in the library."

Vanessa was eating her poached egg greedily. There was a blob of egg yolk at the corner of her mouth. "Rather a treat, this," she said indistinctly. "But not for Peregrine, I'm afraid. He doesn't like to eat until eight. And then, always in the dining room."

"Should I cook something for him?" Angie asked hesitantly, glancing nervously at the mysterious range.

"No, no, my dear," said Woody. "All is prepared. A cold collation awaits Monsieur and Madame in the dining room, beneath a pure white linen cloth. Simply remove the snowy veil, and *voilà!*" He and Vanessa both giggled. They seemed to be looking forward to their outing.

Angie was smoking one cigarette after another. Little pulses seemed to be throbbing all over her, in her wrists, her throat, her stomach. All that she could think of was how soon she would be alone with Peregrine. She was aware of the beating of her heart, and of a pervading sense of delicious apprehension.

She still felt the same when, at half after eight, they were sitting at the long dining-room table, he at its head and she on his right.

He had come into the hall to say good-bye to Vanessa and Woody, and then he and Angie had gone into the library. They had drunk a bottle of

Médoc, and he had opened a second bottle when they went into the dining room. She had removed the cloth from the food on the sideboard, over which hung a painting of a retriever with a bird in its mouth. There was cold beef and a salad for which Peregrine mixed a dressing.

"You're not eating," he said. It was true. She felt as if there were some obstruction in her throat which made it impossible for her to swallow the rare red beef—a food she always had difficulties with, anyway. "You must eat, Angela," he continued, with a little laugh. "You must keep up your strength, you know. You may need it."

She felt the infuriating blush spread over her face. Aware that he was watching her, she took a deep draught from her wine glass. "Steady, girl," he said. "We don't want you to be incapacitated."

It was getting dark outside. On the table, three white candles burned in a branched silver candelabrum. Its mate, unlit, stood at the other end of the table. The three candle flames rose pale and straight in the absolute stillness of the evening.

She couldn't finish the beef, but she managed to eat most of her salad, and then peeled and nibbled at a peach while Peregrine ate bread and cheese.

When they had finished, he stood up. "Coffee in the library," he said. With forefinger and thumb, he pinched out the three candle flames, one by one. "How do you do that without burning your fingers?" she asked as they went into the dimly lit hall. "If you press firmly enough, you don't feel anything," he said.

In one corner of the library, on a low table, was a large silver tray on which were the ingredients for coffee and an electric kettle. He made the coffee, and brought her a cup. "Brandy?" he asked.

"Why, yes," she said. "I think I will."

"I see that I'm corrupting you," he said.

A silence fell as they sipped their coffee and their brandy. She became acutely conscious of his movements. The stirring of his coffee with the little silver-gilt spoon, the measured way he raised his glass to his lips.

She opened a fresh packet of cigarettes. "You smoke too much," he said. "We must do something about that." He stood up, and took her lighter from her. Her eyes met his as he lit the cigarette, which she tried to steady between her fingers. "Your hands are trembling," he said.

"Yes," she answered. "I suppose I'm still a little shaky."

"No brooding, now," he said. "I think some activity is called for." He held out his hand, and helped her to her feet. "Music," he said. Holding her hand loosely in his, he led her to the ballroom. She wandered round the room, humming to herself, as he started the musical box. It played "The Merry Widow," just as it had before, but the music seemed extraordinarily loud and jangling tonight. The light from the chandelier blazed down as he took hold of her, with that iron hand at the base of her spine, and circled, circled, never reversing. She allowed herself to gaze up into his face, impassive above her, with its brilliant eyes. She was breathless. As the waltz ended, she, irresistibly, went limp. But his hand sustained her. "Time for the next activity, Angela," he said. "You're not flagging, are you?"

She was filled with a sudden wild gaiety. "No," she said. "Oh, no."

He released her. "Then the next activity," he said, "shall be hide and seek. Angela, will you play another game of hide and seek with me?"

She glanced toward the door and the shadowy corridor outside, imagined the dimness of the hall beyond, and the dark stairs ascending. But gaiety, and a kind of bravado, welled up powerfully inside her. "Yes," she said. "Yes, I'll play."

The musical box ground into another waltz. Peregrine had started to count, but the music drowned the counting as she ran down the corridor into the hall. The stairs loomed ahead of her. She knew exactly where she was going. And so did he. She felt sure of that, in her bones, in her pounding heart. Up the stairs she hurried, still breathless from the waltz, and flew along the gallery to the grand piano. And, just as she had done before, she crouched in the darkness, clinging to one of the piano's thick legs.

The music stopped. In the sudden silence she heard Peregrine's shout of "Coming!" Then the music started again. A very old tune. What was it? She couldn't remember its name. And now she heard the creak of his tread on the stairs.

She wanted, suddenly, to break the spell, to change the pattern, to stand up, to call out, *It's all right, Peregrine. I'm here. You've won. Let's go back to the library.* The safe, familiar library. But she stayed, crouching by the piano.

She saw the outline of his figure at the top of the stairs. He wasn't singing this time. He was absolutely quiet. Downstairs, the music still jangled, and she still couldn't remember the name of the tune.

Now he was approaching along the gallery, step by step. When he had nearly reached her, she couldn't help giving a little gasp. But this time he didn't skid toward her. He came right up to the piano, and squatted on his haunches in front of her. "Ah," he said, and he took her hand from the leg of the piano, and pulled her gently toward him. He stood up, raising her with him. Now she was held against him, his hand on the base of her spine, just as it had been in the waltz. She closed her eyes. She raised her lips. And, suddenly, the hand at the base of her spine tipped her back onto the floor. Her head cracked violently against the boards. She cried out. He was on top of her. With his left hand he grasped both her wrists and forced them down behind her head. Panicking wildly, she started to kick and struggle. With his right hand, deliberately, he tore her blouse open from neck to waist, tugged at the waist of her skirt, and ripped it down to the hem.

It was rape: savage, ruthless, painful. She couldn't remember ever feeling such pain before. On it went, with ferocious violence. Then he came with a harsh groan. His dead weight crushed her. He released her hands. Her wrists burned.

After a moment he levered himself up on his hand and looked down at her, without expression. The heavy sound of his breathing filled her ears. Then he was looming over her, a knee on either side. She pulled her skirt around her with one hand; with the other she gathered the edges of her torn blouse.

Peregrine smiled. "Rather late for such maiden-ly modesty," he said. "But it's delightful all the same." His voice was cool, detached. "A Victorian

Royal Academy picture," he continued. "Discreetly pornographic."

He stood up, still smiling. Terror possessed her. She clambered to her knees, edged backward, stumbled to her feet, pressing back against the side of the piano. *Escape.* But beyond the piano was the end of the gallery, and in front of her was Peregrine. He took a step forward. Again, he seized her hands.

She was lying on top of the counterpane of the four-poster bed. The sun was shining. The curtains were open, moving slightly in a delicate breeze. She ached and burned all over. She moaned, remembering in a wild speeded-up scramble everything that had happened the night before. She rolled over, burying her face in the counterpane. Unthinkable, unendurable. The games, the gloves and butterflies; all the time, this had been what lay beyond them. The repeated rape in the gallery. The violence and the terror.

She must leave. Leave now. Just as soon as she had the strength. She rolled over, onto her back again. The various aches of her body had a curious fascination. She couldn't resist testing them, the way she remembered once prodding an aching tooth with her tongue. She closed her eyes. The curtains rustled, and she felt the cool touch of the breeze on her face. She could hear the heavy cooing of a dove in the woods. Exerting all her willpower, she opened her eyes and pushed herself up into a sitting position. Then, cautiously, she swung her feet over onto the floor, and stood up. She took off the remnants of her skirt and blouse, which were hanging round her, and pushed them into the bottom drawer of the bow-fronted chest. Then she went into the bathroom, where she bathed in water as hot as she could bear. She brushed her teeth, and splashed herself with Bellodgia, and went back into the bedroom. Out of her suitcase she took a clean white *broderie-anglaise* dressing gown and put it on. Something was worrying her. She gave a little hysterical laugh at the thought. *Everything* was worrying her. But this was something specific.

She groped for it. Then she remembered. She half ran across the room to the door. She took the doorknob in her hand. She hesitated. She wanted to put off finding out if she were right. Then she turned the knob. It twisted uselessly in her hand. Yes, the door was locked.

She remembered Peregrine, guiding her impersonally along the corridor, his hand on her shoulder. He had opened the door of her room and pushed her, quite gently, inside, and closed the door. That was when she had heard the sound of the key turning in the lock, before she staggered over to the bed and sank down on top of it, her mind almost immediately whirling down out of consciousness into sleep. Now, standing with her hand still resting on the doorknob, she tried to grasp the implications of the door's being locked. Peregrine didn't want anyone to know what had happened—that must be it! He would be afraid that she would tell Vanessa. He probably meant to come and sneak her out of the house when no one was about.

She heard footsteps approaching along the corridor. Instinctively, she headed back across the room, to the bed. She dragged back the counterpane, was inside, lying back, pulling the bed-clothes up to her chin, as the key turned in the lock.

It was Woody who came in. He was wearing his blue jeans and a purple T-shirt. He was carrying a tray. As he put it down on the bedside table, she saw that it held a cup of tea and a plate on which was a slice of buttered toast cut into fingers.

"The top of the morning to you," he said in a heavy Irish accent. And then, in his ordinary voice, "And how are you today? I'm a *wreck*, my-self. Bette Davis positively tore my emotions to *shreds*."

Angie was blushing. She could feel that her face was scarlet. Though surely Woody couldn't have any idea of what had happened. But, to open the door, he had had to turn the key in the lock. She put that thought to one side. She reached out desperately for the cup of tea. As she lifted it from the tray, toward her, the cup rattled wildly in the saucer. She lowered it to rest against her chest, and then, with trembling fingers ("Your hands are trembling," Peregrine had said), raised the cup to her lips. The tea was hot and sweet. She gulped it down.

"Oh what a beautiful morning," Woody was caroling, over by the window. A sound at the door made Angie turn her head. Peregrine was stand-ing in the doorway. He wore khaki trousers and a dazzlingly white shirt. *He's come to apologize,* was the thought in her head. She put the cup and saucer carefully down on the tray. Now Woody was moving toward the door.

"Woody," she said, and then, again, "Woody!" But it was as if he didn't hear her. He went past

Peregrine, out of the room, and Peregrine pushed
the door shut behind him.

Half an hour later, she was lying, curled up tightly, trying to think.

He had come over to the bed, without speaking,
without smiling. She had shrunk back, as far as
she could, into the pillows. He stood, looking
down at her, for a moment. Once again she was
struck by his total lack of expression. Then he took
the bedclothes in his hand, and tugged them off
her in one movement. He leaned over, and put a
hand on each side of her waist, and lifted her out
of bed, and put her down on the floor, and
kneeled over her. And then, as before, he took her
wrists in his hand and pinioned them behind her
head.

This time, she didn't resist. She lay absolutely
still, and silent, she thought, except that she heard
a little whimpering sound, and wondered where it
was coming from, and then realized that it came
from her own mouth. On and on went the pain,
until, at last, he came with that harsh groan, and
his weight pressed her into the floor. And then he
was standing up, turning, leaving her laid out on
the floor like a corpse, going out of the room, and
closing the door. She heard the key turn in the
lock.

At last, with a blind, groping movement, she
had raised herself, clutched at the bed, and half
hoisted, half crawled her way up its side. Then she
had dragged the bedclothes up around her head,
burrowing down into them, curling up as tightly
as she could. As if she wanted to disappear into
her own center. *But there seemed to be no center
there.* That was when she had put her thumb in

her mouth, and tried to suck herself down into darkness, her other hand, the while, pinching, pulling, at the sheet.

But now she lay still, and tried to think. She had to try to work it all out, to understand what was happening to her and why she was a prisoner, but none of it seemed to make any sense. What she must do, she decided, was let Peregrine know that she wouldn't put up with any more of it. She would tell him that she wouldn't go to the police, even though she ought to. "But," she heard herself saying, with a cool, controlled little smile, "I've really had quite enough of policemen." And he would set her free.

She got up, and went over to one of the windows, and pushed it wide open. She looked down to where the glass dome of the conservatory curved away from the side of the house. Certainly there was no hope of escape that way. Beyond the conservatory, the pale skeleton of the Weeping Wellingtonia was stark against the yellowing August trees.

She went into the bathroom and washed. She put on blue jeans, a cotton shirt, and sandals. Then she went over to the door. She rattled the handle, and then started to batter on the panels with her fists. She shouted, "Let me out! Let me out!" but her voice sounded shrill and ineffectual. She paused. She couldn't hear a sound from beyond the door. She shouted and banged again until she was exhausted. Then she went over to the bed, and sat down on the edge of it. Suddenly she felt ravenously hungry. She swallowed down the cold greasy fingers of toast on the tray. As she finished, she heard footsteps in the gallery. She was off the bed in a moment, and over by the door, hammering and calling. As the key turned in the lock, she stopped. Involuntarily, she took a step back as the door opened.

Peregrine stood there, and, with a wild rush of courage, she flung herself at him, pushing and pummelling. He stood like a wall, unmoving, immovable, till she raised her right hand to strike at his face, and he grasped her wrist, and twisted it round behind her back.

"You're going to let me out." Her voice sounded like a stranger's, so high and cracked. "You're going to let me out of here."

He smiled then. He shook his head. "Oh, no, Angela," he said. "That's where you're wrong. I'm going to shut you in." And, still holding her wrist, he twisted her round and started to force her across the room. When he opened the closet door, she screamed, "No, no!" but he pushed her inside. The door was shut; the bolt clicked to. She was banging on the door and screaming. "No! No!" in the darkness, till at last she sank down on the floor, and heard the silence.

It was so absolutely quiet, absolutely dark. In fact, she could feel the silence and the blackness pressing down on her like a weight, crushing her, suffocating her. *Suffocating.* The idea made her start pounding on the door again, till she realized how futilely she was using up her energy. And all the time, of course, she must be using up air. How long would the air in the closet last? How she wished she knew something about science! Oxygen, carbon dioxide. The words came into her head but meant nothing, except that she knew that one was good and the other, bad.

Time passed. She found the position she felt safest in—sitting with her hands clasped round her legs, her head resting on her knees. From time to time great shivers ran up her spine. Was she hot or cold? She didn't know.

How long had she been locked in there? As more and more dark silent time passed, she felt herself less and less able to tell, shivering again, kneading her calves with her fingers. She heard herself moaning. They were going to leave her there to die. *Walled up.* She heard the bolt pulled back. The door was opened.

It was Woody, tugging at the shoulder of her blouse, taking her hand, helping her to stand up. "Oh, poor Angie," he was saying. Her rescuer! Who must have just found out what was happening, and had come at once to set her free. He was on her side, then. Now he was patting her arm, and she was crying. He was saying, "There, there. Cheer up now." He produced a handkerchief from the pocket of his jeans, and dabbed at her eyes with a movement that reminded her of the pecking of a hen. She smiled.

"*That's* better," he said. "And now, what next?"

"I must go," she said. "You must help me to get out of here."

He looked at her blankly. "'What next? he repeated. Then he said, "A bath, I think."

"I had a bath this morning," she said stupidly.

"No law that *I've* heard of says you can't bathe twice in one day. You should see yourself, my dear. Goodness knows when that cupboard was last cleaned. Ten-sixty-six, *I* should say, from the look of you. Now, Angie, you just find yourself something clean to put on, and I'll get your bath ready. Then it's straight to beddy-byes for you."

She was too tired to argue. He bustled into the

bathroom, and a moment later she heard the faucets turned on. Mechanically she went over to her suitcase and groped among its contents until she found a clean white nightdress.

"That's right," said Woody. "There's a good girl." Gently he chivied her toward the bathroom. "See you when you've had your bath, dear," he said, closing the bathroom door behind her.

When she came out, the room was empty. The breakfast tray had been removed. Her bed had been neatly made and turned down. She went over to the door, and tried the handle. The door was locked, of course. She'd known it would be. And of course Woody must be in the plot, or whatever it was, even though he seemed such a kind little man.

Wearily, she got into bed. How marvelous it was to sink back against the pillows, stroking the smooth white border of the sheet with her hand. How wonderfully restful—for her body, anyway. Her mind kept spinning round. *Walled up. Ten-sixty-six. I'm going to shut you in.*

The key turned. The door opened, and Woody came in, carrying a tray. He brought it over, and put it down on the bedside table.

"Five thirty," he said. "I didn't know quite what to make you at this time of day. But then I thought, well, how about a nice 'igh tea. Ever so comforting, I always say." There was a big mug of tea on the tray, two boiled brown eggs, thin slices of bread and butter, and a piece of ginger cake.

"A drink," she said. "What I want is a drink."

"Afraid not, dear. Strictly *verboten.*" Woody perched on the side of her bed.

Reluctantly she started on the food, and found that she was ravenous.

"That's the way," said Woody. "*Much* the best thing to do, in the circumstances."

She paused to ask, "But what *are* they?"

"What are what, ducky?"

"The circumstances," she said.

"Goodness, don't ask little me, dear. This isn't *my* show."

"Your *show*?"

"I mean, it's nothing to do with me, none of my business. Let no one ever say Woody was one to poke his nose in uninvited."

"And Vanessa?"

"Oh, I wouldn't worry your head about Vanessa," he said airily. He stood up, and went over to the window. "The evenings are drawing in," he said. "Could that be the last rose of summer I espy in that very untidy flower bed? Well, it may be untidy, but what I always say is 'I'm a good plain cook, but gardening I was *never* hired for.' No, begorrah"—and he switched to an Irish brogue—"there was nothing said about gardening by the masther when he found me, just a sweet colleen in the County Down." He paused. "How I do run on," he said, and glanced at his watch. "I really must dart away now. There's the dinner to prepare. It's as much as my place is worth to stay on gossiping here."

She was lighting a cigarette. He came over to the bed. "There's a good girl," he said. "She's eaten up every mouthful, except her bit of cake! I'll leave that by you, in case you suffer from night starvation, like in the adverts. But now it's time for beddy-byes."

He put his hand in his pocket and produced a small plastic container. Out of it he tapped two shiny red capsules. "Same as the ones you had the other night, dear," he said.

He held them out to her. She hesitated. "Now," he said, "don't you trust me? Oh, you must trust old Woody."

"Yes," she said. She sighed. "I suppose I must," and she took the pills from his hand.

"But not too far," he rattled on. "Never trust anyone too far. Not your nearest and dearest. That's my watchword." He went into the bathroom, and came back with a glass of water. He watched her as she swallowed the pills and drank from the glass.

"And now," he said, picking up the tray, and putting the plate with the cake on it down on the table, "a fond farewell." With the tray poised on his uplifted palm, he pranced toward the door. "Nighty-night," he called. "Sleep tight. Mind the bugs don't bite." The door closed behind him, and the key turned in the lock.

She must have fallen asleep within a few minutes, she realized as she woke to the sun pouring in through the windows, and to Woody, framed in the doorway, another tray in his hands.

"*Good morning, good morning. The best to you each morning.*" He was singing the commercial for some breakfast cereal. He put the tray down beside her—tea, a bowl of Müsli with fruit and nuts in it, and two sardines, neatly shoulder to tail, on a piece of toast. "Oh, and you never ate your cake," he exclaimed. "That I baked with my own dainty hands!"

He went over to the window, and looked out. "How are you feeling today?" he asked.

"Fine," she said, and then laughed, astonished.

But she did feel fine. Refreshed and fully conscious. She sat up in bed, and reached for her cup of tea. Woody was peering at something outside the window. Over on his left, she saw the open door.

She was out of bed in a flash, past Woody and through the door. She was running along the corridor. Behind her she heard his call—reproachful —"Oh, Angie!" Then, as she reached the gallery, she could hear his hurrying steps behind her. She skimmed over the wooden floor to the top of the stairs. She started down them. It was then that she saw Peregrine. He was standing in the hall, by the front door. He was looking at a copy of *The Times*. She took this in in the one second before he abruptly turned his head, and saw her, frozen, on the stairs.

He dropped the newspaper on the floor. Something about the way he moved, the kind of bound with which he reached the stairs, its reflex speed and ferocity, paralyzed her with terror for a moment. Then she turned, to flee back along the passage, but Woody was there, facing her, tentatively trying to restrain her with his hands. "Oh, Angie," he said, with that reproachful note in his voice again. She pushed him. He took a step back as Peregrine seized her shoulders from behind.

"We shall have to keep her in handcuffs if she goes on like this, shan't we, Woody?" Peregrine said. He laughed. Woody hovered there, saying nothing. His expression had become blank.

"All right, Woody," Peregrine said. "I'll take over now." He started to propel her along the passage, holding her ahead of him, controlling her by his grip on her arms. She felt like a puppet. She cast an imploring glance back at Woody, but he looked away and started down the stairs.

They were back in her room. Peregrine kicked the door shut, and turned her to face him.

"You have to *learn*, Angela. That's what you're here for. I shall have to make you learn." He forced her down to the floor. This time he used his hands to wrench her thighs apart. He didn't hold her wrists, and she realized, with a dim shadow of contempt for herself, that she dared not use her hands to attack him. She kept them clenched tightly under her chin.

Now he was standing up, beckoning to her to do the same. She obeyed immediately, automatically, stumbling to her feet. "And now I shall give you time to think things over," he said, and suddenly she knew what he intended. She cried out, "Oh, no, not that. I'll do anything you want, but please not that." He was pushing her across the room. She was in the closet. The door was bolted. Darkness and silence covered her like a shroud.

There she was, but *where* was she? So dark, and that terrible old stale smell. The smell of the closet and the smell of herself. *Into the dark, we all go into the dark. And dark the Sun and Moon.* Was it daytime, or night? It was no time, and she was nothing. *Into the dark.*

She couldn't recognize Woody, for a moment, when he opened the door. She just lay there, and gaped at him. Certainly, she couldn't move. He had to kneel down on the floor and drag her out into the room. But she couldn't stand up. She just half sat, half lay there, on the carpet, as, slowly, awareness of what, where, when, seeped into her mind. It was as if she had been somewhere miles and miles away.

It was dark outside the windows. "Late," she murmured. "Very late. Long time."

"Yes, ducky. Much too late and much too long. But we won't go into all *that* now. This is the first *moment* that I've been allowed up here."

He put his hands under her armpits, and managed to hoist her to her feet, support her over the bed, and then heave her onto it. "Too far," he was muttering. "This time he's really gone too far." Shaking his head, he suddenly reminded her again of the White Rabbit in *Alice*, and she smiled feebly. "That's better," he said. "That's the girl. Smiling through. One thing you've got to say for her—she's got a wonderful sense of humor."

"Dirty," she said. "I'm so dirty."

"Right," he said. "I'm going to get your bath ready now." He glanced toward the door. "But no more Great Escapes, hmm? Today's episode of the *Colditz Story* is over, okay?"

She nodded vaguely. She felt like an old doll, lolling limply in the place where it had been discarded. He went into the bathroom. How would she ever get there? she wondered, listening to the water running. But when he helped her down from the bed, she found that, leaning on him, she could manage. He closed the door, but after she had used the lavatory and drunk two glasses of water, she suddenly felt overcome by panic. "Woody," she called—a shrill loud cry which surprised her. He hurried in. "Woody, don't leave me alone. Don't shut the door."

"Oh, dear me," he exclaimed, "bathing the young ladies was *never* part of my place before!" But he helped her out of her nightdress and into the bath. "Now," he said, "you just relax, and I'll bustle round a bit next door. I'll leave the door open; you just have to call if you want me. But I must make your bed, and unpack that untidy old suitcase of yours."

"No," she said, "no, don't unpack." She couldn't bear the idea of being *settled* in that room. But he said, "Nonsense, ducky. Just you relax, like I said."

So she lay in the bath, letting the hot water lap round her, rubbing herself with the cake of soap, and swirling the water over herself with her hand. Then Woody came back, and helped her out of the bath, and took her towel off the rail. "Good old Woody, head pre at St. Hilary's and every girl's favorite chum," he said as he put the towel round her shoulders. She dried herself, and he handed her a clean nightdress. "This is your last," he said. "I must take a few of your things away, and give them a bit of a wash," he went on. "Especially if you're going to get through them at this rate."

The room was tidy. The bed was made. Her clothes had been put away. When she was in bed, Woody said, "Now I'm just going to pop downstairs and get you a bite to eat.

"No, don't go," she said, and then, "I'm not hungry."

But he shook his head. "You haven't had a thing to eat all day."

"If you must go," she said, "what I really want is a drink. Couldn't you bring me just one?"

But he shook his head again. "*Verboten.* I told you." Carrying her untouched breakfast tray, and with a pile of her dirty clothes over his arm, he went out, locking the door behind him. She just lay there. All she knew was that she longed for a drink. Apart from that, she couldn't think. She couldn't move. Except that her right hand plucked, sporadically, fitfully, at the sheet.

When he came back, he fed her with chicken soup, raising the spoon to her lips, popping little pieces of bread into her mouth. "One for Daddy, and one for Mummy, and one for Woody," he said.

When she had finished, he gave her one of the red capsules. "One will do tonight, I think," he said. "We can't have you getting addicted."

She sank back against the pillows, closing her eyes. "Nighty-night," he said from over by the door. Then she heard him switch off the light. But she opened her eyes, and screamed, "No, don't put it out. Don't leave me in the dark," and he turned it on again.

She woke suddenly, her eyes blurred, her head throbbing. She knew at once that someone was in the room, and then she became aware that Peregrine was standing beside the bed. He was unscrewing the shade from the bedside light. He put the shade down on the table, and then he changed the bulb. Why was he doing that? she wondered.

Her blank gaze traveled round the room. On the left, over near the wall, she saw a small waist-high wooden table which hadn't been there before, and drawn up to it, with its back to her, was a wooden chair. On the table were a decanter, with dark liquid in it, and a glass.

Peregrine switched on the bedside lamp. She blinked. Unshaded, the new bulb was of dazzling brightness. He picked up the lamp by its base, and carried it, with its long flex trailing on the floor, over to the wooden table, where he put it down.

The light blazed on the wallpaper, showing its trellises and flowers in brilliant relief.

He came over to the bed again and stood looking down at her. "Up," he said. She didn't move. Dumbly, she shook her head.

"Up," he said again, and stretched out his hand to her. She took it—it felt so cool and impersonal —and he pulled her to her feet, and led her across the room.

"Here," he said, and stood her in front of the wall, behind the table. The unshaded bulb glared in her face. He went over to the door, and switched off the center light. Then he came and sat down at the table. But, after a moment, he glanced round the room, and then stood up again. He went over to the wall where the engraving of the girl with the lamb hung. He unhooked it, and brought it back to the table. He propped it against the lamp so that on his side of the table the bulb was shaded. Then he sat down again, facing Angie. He filled the glass from the decanter. Ruby red, the wine gleamed like a jewel in the light. He sipped it. Dazzled, she couldn't see his face.

"And now, Angela," he said, "you are going to answer some questions."

TWO

"So when did you first fail, Angela?" he asked.

"Fail?" she repeated stupidly. The light was so bright in her eyes. Her head was still throbbing, and the sleeping pill had left a dull, stale taste in her mouth.

"Yes, I want you to tell me which was the first of your failures."

"But why do you say I've failed?" she asked him.

His hands raised the glass to his lips again. "It is I who am asking the questions, not you," he said. "And I asked you when you first failed."

"I've never thought of things in terms of failure," she said.

"No," he agreed. "I'm quite sure that you haven't. I'm quite sure, in fact, that you have systematically evaded doing so. But there comes a time for an end to evasion. Must I repeat my question, Angela?"

She was silent.

"I notice that you're not being cooperative, Angela. I must warn you, if you're not cooperative, then I shall have to lock you up again."

She shrank back against the wall. "Oh, no," she said. "Please not that."

"Stand away from the wall, Angela, and stand up straight. That's right. Very well, I am prepared to help you a little. Let me put the question somewhat differently. What did you do after your father's death?"

"After my father's death?"

"Yes. Please don't keep repeating what I say, like a parrot. What did you do after your father's death, Angela? Think carefully."

She was silent again. But fear of the closet, of the darkness, drove her to speak. She said, "I had a breakdown."

"You escaped, you mean. You couldn't face up to things. And so you failed your father."

"Oh, no," she said. "No, I didn't do that."

"But of course you did, Angela. Your father expected a great deal from you. And as soon as he was dead, you let him down."

"No, I didn't," she said. "I didn't do that. It was only for a short time that I was ill. Then I got better. And after that, I did everything that my father had wanted. I learned about the things that interested him. I went to university, just as he'd planned."

"Leaving your mother to bear her last illness alone. Did your father plan that?"

"Oh, how can you say such a thing? I didn't know that she was dying."

"Didn't you, Angela? Didn't the doctor warn you?"

"I can't imagine," she said, "where you heard all these distorted things about me."

"No arrogance, please, Angela. Do you remember what I warned you about?"

"Yes," she said. "Yes." And she added, "I'm sorry."

"Very well, Angela. You are excused this time, but let's have no more talk of distortions. I know everything about you, Angela. I know far more about you than you know yourself."

He paused. Then he said, "We shall leave the question of your mother, for the moment. You went to university?"

"Yes," she said, "I did."

"Just as your father had planned that you should do?"

"Yes."

"And how long did you stay at university?"

"For a year," she said.

"Did your father intend you to go to university for only a year?"

She raised her hand to shield her eyes from the dazzling light.

"Put your hand down, Angela, and answer my question."

"He didn't say."

"I see. 'He didn't say.' Let me put that question another way. Didn't your father expect you to take a degree?"

"Well, yes, I suppose so," she faltered.

"Ah! You suppose so. So why didn't you?"

"Because I got married," she said.

"You got married. And why did you 'get married' so impetuously?"

She was silent. Then she said, "Because I fell in love."

"And the person you 'fell in love' with—was he the kind of man of whom your father would have approved?"

She groped for an answer. "Well . . . . I suppose I

would say no now. But then I didn't know what he was like."

"You didn't know what he was like. And yet you married him. You abandoned all the plans your father had made for you. Were you happy with this man?"

"Oh, no." She shook her head emphatically. "Never."

"Did you try to make the marriage work?"

"Yes," she said.

"But you didn't succeed?"

"No."

"I see. So what happened next?"

"We started to lead our own lives."

"Were you unfaithful to him?"

"Not until after he became involved with that woman."

"But surely, essentially, you had rejected him long before that?"

"It was he who rejected me. I realized that he had only married me for my money."

"Your father's money, Angela. Anyway, you realized he'd only married you for money. Why didn't you recognize that earlier? Your father arranged for you to inherit all his money when you were eighteen. Is that right?"

"Yes." Again her hand crept up to shield her eyes, but before it reached them, she let it drop to her side.

"Remarkable evidence of his trust in you. Yet you didn't even finish the degree he wanted you to take. And you threw yourself at the first fortune hunter who crossed your path."

"It wasn't like that."

"It wasn't? Oh, I think it was, Angela. I think it

was just like that. You betrayed your father's trust."

"I didn't. I didn't."

"Oh, yes, you did. You betrayed your father's trust. Admit it now."

"No, I won't. I won't."

"You betrayed his trust."

"I didn't."

That was when he stood up.

After the glaring light, the absolute darkness. And darkness rising in her mind, to meet the outer darkness, and to merge with it. *You betrayed your father's trust.*

"I didn't, I didn't." She hammered on the door of the closet with her fists.

When Woody opened the door, and started to fuss round her, like a nanny, it was broad daylight. The table and chair had gone. The picture was back on the wall. The lamp, its shade restored, was on the bedside table again. Woody was tugging at her hand.

"I didn't, Woody," she said. "I didn't."

"Now, come on, Angie," Woody coaxed. "Up you get, ducky. It's bath time now. And then you shall have a nice rest in bed, and I'll bring you ever such a lovely breakfast. 'Higgledy Piggledy, my black hen. She lays eggs for gentlemen.' And for ladies, too, I'll have you know."

She let him lead her into the bathroom. "I didn't, Woody," she said. "I didn't."

"Now, come along, Angie. . . . There's a good girl."

She lay back in the water. If only she could sink

in it, drown in it. Her hair would float on the surface of the water, like Ophelia's.

"Out you get, now." Woody was standing by the bath, holding the big towel. She got out, and he put it round her. "Now I'll fetch your breakfast," he said.

Drying herself, she wandered through into the bedroom, dropped the towel on the carpet, and put on the newly washed nightdress Woody had laid out for her. She was about to get into bed, but then she picked up the towel from the floor, and took it back into the bathroom, and hung it neatly on the rail.

She was in bed when Woody came with her tray. "I hung up the towel," she said as he came in.

"What?" he said, looking puzzled, and then, "Oh, thanks very much."

"At least I'm almost sure I did," she added. "But perhaps I ought to get up and make certain."

"Oh, Angie, what are you on about?" he said. "Just you sit back, and relax, and eat up your breakfast."

How pretty the tray looked! Tears came into her eyes at the sight of the speckled brown egg, the flowered cup and saucer, the dear little fingers of toast. There was even a pink rosebud, in a tiny vase, next to the white linen napkin.

"How can you be so kind to me," she asked, "when he's so cruel?"

"Peregrine, you mean?" Woody said. She looked nervously toward the door, as if the mention of his name might summon him, like a genie in a fairy tale. Then she nodded.

"Oh, Peregrine isn't really cruel," Woody said. "He likes to get his own way, though, and he always does, sooner or later. So it isn't wise to fight him, Angie."

"He's cruel," she said, shaking her head. "He told me that I betrayed my father's trust."

"Eat up your breakfast, ducky," Woody said. Obediently, she cracked the top of tthe egg with the pointed silver spoon, and started to pull off the little pieces of shell. "My father always used to slice off the tops of his eggs," she said. "I tried to do it that way, too, but I could never get it right."

Woody sat down on the end of the bed. "I owe everything to Peregrine, you know," he said. "Saved me from the gutter and a life of shame, you could say."

"And made you his servant?" Angie asked.

Woody flushed. "I'm no servant," he said. "Not really. More a member of the family. Now, my dad, he was a sort of servant. He was the game-keeper here, in the time of old Sir Palfrey, Pere-grine's father. Sir Palfrey was good to me, too. Rescued me from the clutches of my dad. Oh, An-gie—how I did hate that man! And the detestation was mutual, I can assure you of that. He used to take me to this terrible place in the woods. The gamekeeper's larder, they call it, where the game-keeper hangs up the birds of prey he's killed. As a warning to the others. I used to cry when he took me there, and, what's more, when he shot rabbits. It used to drive him mad with anger. He'd beat me, and he'd say, 'You sissy boy! I'm going to make a man of you if it kills me.' Though it was much more likely to have killed me than him, I'm sure."

He broke off. "Angie, what *are* you doing?" She had gathered together all the little pieces of eggshell. She had put them in the egg cup, and had placed the uncracked half of the shell on top, so that the egg looked just like new. And then she had taken a tissue from the box on the bedside table, and had spat into it, and was rubbing a stain of egg yolk from the plate.

"I was just making things tidy," she said. "Go on, Woody. Go on telling me about your father."

"He used to grumble about me to Sir Palfrey. They had long talks together—tramping round the estate, you know. He was an easygoing old fellow, Sir Palfrey. Always had a pleasant word for everyone. Lived in terror of his wife, though. Peregrine's mother. Now she was a Tartar, and no mistake. Ruled the household with a rod of iron. Everyone except Peregrine, that is. He was her one soft spot. Whereas Sir Palfrey, I always felt, really preferred Piers, the younger son. The one that's a professor, and that Peregrine never could stand. Old Lady Donnisthorpe never had much time for Piers, either. Very hard, she was. You would have thought Sir Palfrey might have been relieved when she died. But not a bit of it. A lot of the life seemed to go out of him. Anyway, to get back to what I was saying, Sir Palfrey used to tell my dad to go easy on me. 'We're not all the same, you know, Ashwood,' he'd say, and he started to take a kind of interest in me. I was a bright little lad then. Did well at school. Not that my dad cared anything for that. In fact, it was another black mark against me, so far as he was concerned. But Sir Palfrey, he encouraged me. He talked my dad into letting me take up the scholarship I won to the grammar school, and he paid for my uniform, too. My dad would never have gone

against what Sir Palfrey wanted, which was lucky
for me. Though I didn't turn out such a wonderful
scholar in the end. I got theater-mad, you see, and
all I could think about was plays. I made a lovely
little Juliet; ever so many people said so. Though
some laughed, of course. But not Sir Palfrey. He
came to see the play, and not long after that, he
took me up to London for the day. To see *Romeo
and Juliet*. At the Old Vic, I think it was. He gave
me lunch first, at some place where they carved
great joints of meat on a trolley. But I was so
excited I could hardly eat a thing. Well, anyway,
when he dropped me at home that night, and I
thanked him, he said, 'Well, George,'—George, I
ask you! Hardly *me*, was it? Harry, England, and
St. George, et cetera—'if you're ever in difficulties,
come up to the Hall and see me.' And that was
what I did—though in fear and trembling—when I
decided I wanted to go on the stage. And he
helped me. Brought my dad round to the idea,
and spoke to someone he knew, and got me this
job as general dog's-body in a touring company.
Run by one of the last of the old ranters. Oh, you
should have seen him leaping into the grave in
Hamlet. That was something to see in a man of his
age. His joints used to crack like pistol shots. I'd
be giggling like a mad thing in the wings. Page,
that was me in those days. Enter Page. I didn't
have the height for servingman or man-at-arms.
But I did love the life. Until I had my trouble."

"Your trouble?" Angie asked, shifting the cup
and saucer on the tray so that they were the same
distance from the plate as was the vase with the
rose in it, on the other side.

"There really was a law against it in those
days," Woody said. "And 'gay' meant a lot of

peasants doing folk dances. Well, to cut a long story short, it happened in Bristol. We were playing at that lovely old Theater Royal. And one evening, after the show, I and another boy from the company got mixed up with some sailors—merchant navy, they were. And we were caught, and I ended up inside for a year—well, I actually served nine months. I was quite a pretty boy, in those days, believe it or not, and I really had a bad time with those disgusting old lags. When I came out, I was ever so bitter. That was when I took to the drink. I was working as a washer-up in a London hotel, and spending every penny on the booze. I was sleeping rough. And one night—it was winter, and terribly cold—I was under those arches at the back of the Savoy, where a bit of warmth comes up from the gratings. And who should walk past but Peregrine. In evening dress, he was. If I hadn't been so pissed—"

"Titus," Angie murmured. She was sweeping toast crumbs and salt into a little pile with her finger.

"What? Well, as I say, if I hadn't been so pissed, I never would have spoken, but I piped up, 'Hullo, Master Peregrine.' And he came over—he was very young in those days, Angie, and I don't think anyone's ever been more handsome—and he looked at me, and he said, 'Good God, it's little George.' 'They call me Woody now, Master Peregrine,' says I. 'And I'm Sir Peregrine,' says he. 'My father died six months ago.' 'Well, I'm really sorry to hear that,' says I. 'And I'm sorry to see you in this condition,' says he. And then he just kind of swept me up, and into a taxi, and took me on the train back here, to Foxers. People did look at me askance in the first-class, I must say. I was a right mess, and drunk to boot. But nobody said a word, me being with Peregrine.

"My father had been pensioned off. Living with his sister the other side of Ipswich. Well, I was thankful to hear that, I can tell you. There'd been a lot of changes since the old man died. Everyone thought there was plenty of money, but there turned out to be hardly any. All the servants were gone, except the old butler, Mr. Rolf, and a couple of women who came in from the village to clean.

"It was Peregrine who cured me. Got me off the drink. And that was quite a job, I can tell you. At one time I was seeing things. *DT*'s, you know. And all I wanted was to get at a bottle. But Peregrine put a stop to that. And I came through, and then I began to make myself useful about the place. And after that, there was the war, and Peregrine went off to the army. He got me an exemption. Working on the land, you know. And I had foot trouble, too. Fallen arches. 'I love to dance, but oh my feet,' as the ballerina said. I had to cope with everything. Mr. Rolf was getting quite gaga. He died in the third year of the war."

"And you've been here ever since," Angie said.

"That's right. When Peregrine married Vanessa, I wondered how it would work out. But she fitted in, all right." He sighed. "Well, I must be getting along," he said. "I'm afraid I can't sit here chatting to you all day. Why, what ever would happen to everything? They could never manage without me, you know," he said proudly as he picked up the tray.

When he had gone, she got up and straightened the picture of the girl with the lamb. She had noticed while Woody was talking that it was hanging crookedly. Then she went back to bed, and fell asleep.

She dreamed that she was coming down the stairs of her father's house in Cleveland, and that she went into his library. Her father's desk and chair stood as they had always stood. Everything was the same. Except that her father wasn't there. Was he hiding from her somewhere? She looked behind the curtains and behind the door. Then she noticed that the books in one of the bookcases were false. Her fingers felt for a hidden catch, and found it, and the panel of books swung open. She was in the library at Foxers, and her father was sitting at Peregrine's desk, in the red chair. "Daddy," she exclaimed. Filled with joy, she ran toward him . . . and woke as Woody came in with her lunch tray.

She slept again in the afternoon. When she woke, she went into the bathroom, and scrubbed her hands with the nail brush. Woody found her there. He looked at the reddened skin of her hands, and shook his head. "Back to bed, Angie," he said. "But my hands aren't clean," she replied, still scrubbing. "Of course they are," he said. "I shall confiscate that nailbrush if you don't come back to bed at once." If he took the brush away, she would never be able to get her hands clean. Reluctantly, she rinsed them under the tap, and dried them, half expecting they would leave black fingerprints on the towel. But Woody was right. They did seem to be clean.

She ate the supper Woody brought her, and he took away the tray. He didn't give her pills, or say good night, so she supposed he must be coming back later. It was beginning to get dark.

But with the darkness came Peregrine. Carrying the table in front of him. Putting it down, facing the wall. Going out of the room, and coming back, a moment later, with the chair. Out again, and back with the decanter and the glass, which he placed on the table. Coming over to the bed, and unscrewing the shade of the lamp.

"No," she said, but he carried the lamp over to the table, and fetched the picture from the wall, and propped it against it.

"Up," he said. And she got up, and he pointed, and she went and stood by the wall, and the light dazzled her eyes.

"Now, where were we?" he said, in the shadow, sipping from his glass. And then, "Oh, yes. You betrayed your father's trust."

"But I didn't," she said.

"We shall proceed from there, Angela. Please don't try to defy me. Or you know what will happen."

She was silent.

"Your husband," Peregrine said, "committed a crime. What was your response?"

"My response?"

"Don't parrot me, Angela. You called the police, I believe."

"I called for help."

"You called for help. And help came. And, as soon as you could, you fled."

"I went to a hotel. There were reporters all around the house."

"You went to a hotel. And what happened then?"

"Well, I talked to the police, and to other people."

"And after that?"

"I . . . broke down."

"You escaped again, you mean. Again, you evaded."

"Oh, I must wash my hands," she said. "They are so dirty. I must go and wash my hands. Please let me go and wash my hands."

"Angela, stay where you are. I warn you not to move."

She sagged against the wall.

"Stand up, Angela," he said. "Take one pace forward." And she took a faltering forward step.

"You betrayed your husband," he said. "Just as you betrayed your father."

"No."

"You escaped. You evaded. Until everything was easy again. With that little Jew pouncing round you, telling you you were wonderful."

"He didn't. If you mean Dr. Blaumann. He never told me I was wonderful."

"But he sympathized with you, in your sad plight."

"He helped me."

"He helped you to escape from facing the truth. No wonder, when you were paying him so much money. Oh, Angela, how easy it has always been for you to escape."

"I want to wash my hands."

"Miss Pontius Pilate. You want to wash your hands of yourself. Don't try to deceive me. I'm not some pathetic little money-grubbing refugee."

"He isn't. He's a famous doctor."

"And do you think your 'famous doctor' would have been so concerned about you if you'd been poor? Would he have had all that time to spend on you, do you think, if you'd been a patient on our wonderful National Health Service?"

"That didn't arise."

"No, of course, Angela, it didn't arise. Has anything ever arisen? one wonders. Except finding a way out?" He paused. He took another sip of wine. "Well, let us change our ground," he said. "What happened next? Under Dr. Blaumann's ministrations, you ... got better, as you would probably put it. Is that so?"

"Yes," she said. "I got better."

"And what happened then?"

"I wanted a new life."

"Ah, a new life. Off with the old and on with the new. And what was this new life that you decided on?"

"I wanted to do something different. On my own."

"Ah, yes. And what did this 'something different' consist in?"

"I thought I'd try to write a book."

"And what kind of book did you choose to write?"

"I wanted to write ... some fairy stories."

"Ah, very interesting. Some fairy stories." He took a sip from his glass. "And you found a fairy-tale cottage to write your fairy stories in?"

"I found a cottage."

"Yes. And once you were in your fairy-tale cottage, did you start to write your fairy stories?"

She hesitated. "Yes."

"And how successful were you?"

"Successful?"

"In writing them?"

She faltered. "So many things ... happened."

"Things happened, did they? And where did they happen? In your head, 'Angela. You made them happen. Didn't you? You made them happen." He drank from his glass. "Once again you couldn't face reality. Not even the reality of writing fairy stories in a fairy-tale cottage. So, once again, Angela, you betrayed your father's trust."

"No, it's not true. It's not true. If my father were here," she screamed, "he would never let you talk to me like this."

"But your father isn't here, Angela," he said. "Your father's dead. Killed by the way in which, when you were fourteen, you betrayed him. That was the first of your many betrayals, Angela."

"No, he forgave me. He forgave me." But now Peregrine was forcing her toward the closet.

Woody opened the door. His face looked gray in the gray daylight. She was ashamed. Her nightdress was soaked with urine. Piss, Jessica would have said. And she started, at once, to crawl toward the bathroom on ther hands and knees.

But Woody barred the way, shaking his head, a finger on his lips. She stared up at him. "I can't talk to you," he whispered. "But you aren't allowed in there. Not now."

He was holding a glass of water. He knelt down beside her, putting it to her lips. She gulped the water down. "More," she murmured. But he shook his head again. He did not meet her eyes as he stood up. He went over to the door. It closed behind him. She heard the key turn in the lock.

The table and chair were still there, facing the wall. The half-empty decanter, the glass, and the unshaded lamp, switched off now, with the picture propped against it, still stood on the table. Through the open curtains she could see gray sky. She started to crawl toward the bathroom again, but then she heard the key, and stayed quite still.

Peregrine came in. As on previous occasions, she was struck by the cleanness of his shirt, snowy white and crisply ironed. He came over, and stood looking down at her.

"What a state you're in, Angela," he said. "You'd like a bath, I'm sure."

She nodded her head.

"There's no reason why you shouldn't have one," he said. Then he turned, and went over to the table, and switched on the lamp. He went over to the window and drew the curtains. It was night again. "If you behave reasonably, that is," he said. "Come." He gestured with his hand toward the table.

"I can't," she said. "I can't." But he came over, and took her hand, and half dragged her to her feet, and she staggered after him, over to the wall, and slumped against it, the light burning in her eyes. Her eyes ached so much. She closed them.

"Stand up, Angela," he said. "Open your eyes."

She forced her eyes open. She tried to stand away from the wall, but her shoulders sagged back against it.

"Very well," he said. "That will do." He sat down in the chair. "And now," he said, "we shall have to go back to the beginning." He paused before he spoke again: "You have failed at everything you have ever undertaken, Angela."

She was silent.

"Is that true, Angela? Answer me. You have failed at everything you have ever attempted."

"I don't know." She heard her voice rise in a wail.

"You don't know. Well, let us itemize it all once again. You betrayed your father, before and after his death. You defied him, and then, after he was dead, you escaped from recognizing the truth about his death."

She did not utter.

He went on. "Then you deserted your mother, whom your father had left in your care."

"He didn't say so."

"He didn't say so. But he had always looked after her. He would never have abandoned her in her last illness. And he would not have expected you to do so."

"He wanted me to go to university," she said.

"Yes, he did. And you went to university. For one year. And then you married, on impulse. And then you failed in your marriage. And you failed your husband. And you escaped from life just as you had done after your father died. And then you decided on a different escape. Into the world of fairies."

"Stop," she moaned. "Please stop."

"No, Angela, we shall continue. You couldn't even face up to a fairy-tale world. You invented a series of preposterous events which excused you even from that. Isn't it true, Angela?"

"I don't know." Again she heard her voice rise in that high wail.

"You *do* know. Angela, I am not being unreasonable. You have every chance to explain yourself. You have all the time in the world. Just tell me, Angela, one thing you have done; one thing at which you have not failed."

Her mind darted, then cringed back, like a rat in a maze. "I don't know," she said again. Then, "I'm too tired. I can't think."

There was a pause. Then he asked quietly. "What are your plans, Angela?"

"My plans?"

"Why, yes. What are your plans for the future? What do you intend to do with the rest of your life?"

"I don't know. I don't know. I want to sleep."

"The sleeping beauty. Sleeping her life away. Is that the best answer you can produce, Angela? If it is, then your life means nothing."

Darkness welled up inside her. "Nothing," she echoed.

He leaned forward across the table. "And what would your father have thought about that, Angela? Your father, who expected so much from you, and who wanted you to have everything."

"Whom her father loves so well," she murmured.

"What? Yes, your father loved you, Angela. And you would have disappointed him. Admit it, Angela. That's the least you can do. Admit it. He would have wanted you to do that, at least."

The darkness was all round her now. Even the blazing light seemed to have a core of blackness.

"You failed, Angela. Admit it for your father's sake."

For your father's sake, the darkness echoed.

"I failed," she said.

"You failed, and your life is empty."

"My life is empty."

"You betrayed your father's trust."

Suddenly, sobs shook her. Her shoulders heaved. A howl came from her mouth. "I betrayed his trust!" And she sank to the floor, and crouched there, howling, weeping, her head bowed to the ground, her body rocking forward and back. The tears were dripping into her filthy nightdress. "I betrayed his trust!" And now her wailing and rocking were a gale.

She raised her head. Where was he? The light on the table had been turned off. A faint glimmer of daylight came through the curtains. And more light was coming from the bathroom, where she could hear water flowing and splashing.

She was still crying, but with little gasping grunts now, as if a machine were running down. The sound of water stopped. She saw Peregrine silhouetted in the bathroom doorway. Then he came toward her, and she shrank away. But he was at the table, pouring wine from the decanter into the glass, bringing it over to her, kneeling down beside her, putting his arm round her shoulders, and holding the glass to her lips.

"Drink," he said. She drank. The wine tasted strange in her mouth, as if she had never tasted wine before. A little of it trickled down her chin. He took a handkerchief from his pocket, and wiped her face; the wine from her lips, the tears from her cheeks. Then he put the wineglass down on the floor.

His arms were round her. He was gathering her up so gently, carrying her toward the bathroom, smiling down into her face. "Angela, my poor little Angie," he was saying. "Everything is going to be all right now. Everything is going to be all right."

He stood her on the bath mat. He pulled her nightdress over her head, and tossed it into a corner. Now he was lifting her into the bath. He was washing her all over, soaping her facecloth, wringing it out. How filthy the water was becoming. There were purple cramp marks on her calves.

He lifted her out, and sat her down on the bath mat. Now he was letting the water gurgle away down the drain, taking all the vileness with it. And now he was turning on the taps again, taking her bottle of Bellodgia from the shelf and shaking it into the water. He tested the temperature of the water with his hand. He turned off the faucets and lifted her into the bath again, into the hot scented water. "Lie back," he said, and pulled her down in the water. She clutched at the side of the bath. He laughed. "Silly girl," he said. "Did you think I was going to drown you? Oh, no, Angela, I have very different plans." He laughed again. His eyes were sparkling. She couldn't help smiling, and then, suddenly, she couldn't help blushing, too. "Little Angie's famous blush," he said. One of his hands was behind her head. With the other, he was using the cake of soap to wash her hair. "Shut your eyes," he said. "We don't want to make you cry."

She closed her eyes. Gently, he tilted her head back again. *Her hair was floating on the surface of the water, like Ophelia's.* And now he was lifting her out of the bath, standing her on the mat, rubbing her hair dry with the big towel, and then wrapping her in the towel and patting and rubbing her all over. She felt a glow spread over the surface of her skin.

He let the towel fall to the ground, and lifted her up, naked, and carried her, her cheek pressed against his damp shirt front, into the dim bedroom.

"My nightdress," she murmured as they reached the bed.

"You don't need it," he said.

She was between the sheets, and he was taking off his clothes, letting them drop to the floor.

She woke in the darkness, starting, trembling, stretching her hand out toward the bedside lamp that wasn't there. His hand came over and took hers, and pulled her round to face him. He kissed her lips, and then drew back and smiled. He put a finger across the base of her throat, and stroked up toward her chin, as one strokes a cat. And like a cat, she wanted to purr. Everything had changed.

"But why," she said slowly, "why did you torture me like that?"

"I had to," he said, still stroking her neck from throat to chin. "It was the only way to make you understand."

"To make me understand?" she repeated after him.

"To make you understand the truth," he said. "And to set you free." Now he was smoothing the damp tangles of her hair. "But that's all over now. Though we shall have to talk a lot, in quite a different way." He paused. He laughed. He said, "But not now."

He was making love to her again. She was clinging to him, breathless. The princess was waking from her long sleep. How could he be the same person. . . . But the thought was left unfinished. She was laughing, murmuring, crying out. She was drowned, lost, found at last.

She woke. It was morning, and Peregrine had gone. Sunlight was glinting round the edges of the curtains. Slowly, she got out of bed. She stretched. She went over to the windows, and drew back the curtains. The leaves of the trees were yellow, and a yellowish green. Pale, the Weeping Wellingtonia reared its dinosaur head. She went over to the door and tried the handle. Yes, the door was locked. Then she realized that she didn't care. Would she mind, she wondered, staying in this room forever? Now. She thought of Rapunzel, in the witch's tower, letting down her plait of hair for the Prince to climb each evening.

She wandered round the room. She touched the wall against which she had stood. The trellises and flowers on the wallpaper had become her garden, her bower. She sat down in the chair where Peregrine had sat, and rested her cheek against the table. She stood up, and picked up the picture of the girl with the lamb and hung it in its place on the wall, where a square of wallpaper was paler than the rest. She carried the lamp back to the bedside table, and screwed on its shade.

She stared at her reflection in the mirror. Her face was pale; her lips were swollen; her eyes were reddened and shadowed. Her hair rioted in wild tendrils. "I had to make you understand the truth," he had said. "And to set you free." She ran her hands down her naked body, and saw her blush reflected in the dim speckled glass.

She bathed. She brushed her teeth. She put on a clean nightdress, smiling. ("My nightdress." "You don't need it.") She stood in front of the mirror, brushing her hair. Behind her, the door opened. Spellbound, she gazed into the mirror, her hand arrested in midair. But it was Woody whom she saw reflected in the depths of the glass, holding a tray. "Woody," she said, turning round and smiling at him. "Woody, how nice to see you."

"Well, well!" he said. "You are looking pleased with yourself this morning, I *must* say."

She laughed. She came toward him. "Breakfast?" she said. "I'm starving. What have you brought me this morning? I could eat a horse."

"If only I'd known," he said, "I would have been off to the farm with my tiny catapult. As it is, I'm afraid there's only eggs and bacon."

"Marvelous," she said, and sat down at the little table with the tray. She tried not to attack the food too ravenously—how delicious it tasted—but she had finished everything—the eggs, the bacon, the toast, washed down with great gulps of tea—in a few minutes.

"Well," Woody exclaimed, coming in from the bathroom, where he'd been tidying up, "you were certainly right about your appetite!"

Dear Woody. Now he was making her bed. How kind he was. All the same, she wasn't sorry when, taking the tray, he bustled away. She heard the key turn. She thought, *But I don't care.*

Her eyes ached a little. *From the tears she'd shed.* Suddenly she felt weak and exhausted. She decided that she could sleep a little more.

When she woke, Peregrine was standing looking down at her. He was smiling. She stretched out her hand to him, and he took it, and sat down on the side of the bed.

"You've slept well?" he asked.

"Mmm," she said. "So well." She lifted his hand and rubbed it against her cheek and across her lips. He smiled again. Then, gently, he took his hand away.

"It's time to work," he said. "I can't allow you to be lazy."

"Work?" she said, raising her eyebrows.

"Yes, Angela," he said. "We have work to do. You have to think, Angela. We have to talk."

"Oh," she said. "Oh, yes." She smiled.

"You must be serious, Angela," he said. "Now, come on. Sit up. Don't flop there." Obediently she hoisted herself up against the pillows. "That's better," he said. "But sit upright."

She leaned forward. His eyes were fixed on her face. He wasn't smiling now, and his gaze was so piercing that she turned her head aside.

"Look at me, Angela," he said. He took one of her hands in each of his. She forced herself to meet his eyes.

"It was all true, Angela, wasn't it?" he said.

"All true." Eagerly she nodded.

"Now, don't be sloppy, Angela." His tone was curt. "*What* was all true?"

"Why, everything you said," she answered.

"Don't give me answers that you think will please me." Now his voice was cold. "I'm talking," he went on, "about the things *you* said. The things you recognized and admitted."

"Must we talk about all that now?" She smiled. She widened her eyes and fluttered her lashes.

"Perhaps I'm making a mistake," he said, "Talking to you here, like this. Perhaps I should tell you to get up, make you go and stand over there by the wall again."

"Oh, no," she said. "Please." And then, "You promised."

"Well then, you must concentrate," he said.

"I will." Solemnly, now, she nodded.

"It's true that you've failed, isn't it?" he said.

"I've failed," she echoed.

"Failed at everything. You recognize that."

"Yes."

"Really recognize it?"

"Yes, I have failed at everything."

"And you have always tried to escape from reality, and have refused to face it?"

"Yes, I've tried to escape. I've refused to face things."

"You really recognize that?"

"Yes, I really do."

"And by failing and escaping, you truly admit that you betrayed your father's trust."

She shivered. Could she really say those words again, here, in the daylight, her hands held in Peregrine's? She was silent.

"You betrayed your father's trust," he repeated. And the tone in which he spoke chilled her. She suddenly felt that there was a wall of ice between them, separating them. Or an abyss on whose brink she was poised, the darkness rising up from it to engulf her.

"I betrayed," she said, and then, ". . . my father's trust." Now the tears were in her eyes. They were trickling down her cheeks, and she couldn't brush them away, because her hands were clasped in his.

"So your life," he said, "has had no meaning."

"My life has had no meaning." The tears were flowing faster now, unchecked.

"Hush, Angela," he said. "The question is, what are you going to do about it? That is what you have to think about now. What are you going to do, Angela?"

She was still crying. "I don't know."

"You're trying to escape again. But I'm not going to let you do that. Am I?

"You're not going to let me." And, curiously, as she said the words, she felt a little better.

"I am going to help you."

"You are going to help me." Her voice was firmer now.

"To start again."

"To start again."

"You are going to have a purpose in life, Angela. A new purpose," he said.

"I am?"

"Repeat it after me, Angela. You are going to have a new purpose in life."

"I am going to have a new purpose in life."

"And what is that purpose going to be?"

"I don't know," she faltered, but the tears were drying on her cheeks.

"You are going to accomplish a mission, Angela."

"To accomplish a mission."

"And you are going to be worthy of your father's trust, at last. You are going to fulfill all his expectations. Repeat that, Angela."

"I am going to be worthy of my father's trust, at last. I am going to fulfill all his expectations."

She felt the tension in his hands as they gripped hers more tightly. "You are going to build a glorious future," he said. "Founded on the great heritage of the past."

What could he be talking about? But she was wholly possessed now by the blaze in his eyes, the mounting exhilaration of his voice.

"You are going to become a part of history," he said.

Why should she have a sudden vision of all those tombs in the church at Clave? Then it was gone, as he raised her hands within his. He held them clasped, as in a pledge, between them.

"We are going to restore my house to its former splendor, Angela," he said. "You and I. Stone by stone. Wall by wall. Tree by tree."

The cherubs on the ballroom ceiling suddenly appeared before her eyes, grew brilliant as she looked at them: flesh and gold and crimson against a sky of richly clouded blue. The perfect lusters on the chandelier tinkled in a sudden gust of wind. Outside, the lawns were swaths of green velvet, and the great iron gates swung open as she and Peregrine went through them.

"Stone by stone. Wall by wall. Tree by tree," he repeated. "You and I."

And, "Stone by stone," she said. "Wall by wall. Tree by tree. You and I."

His voice was softer now. "We shall do so many things together, Angela. Such important things. But not just for ourselves. For future generations. We shall restore this house together, Angela, you and I. But you are going to do something greater still.

"Angela," he said. "You are going to have my child. You are going to bear my son."

THREE

Down the stairs she came, in floating green, her hand resting on Peregrine's arm. Down in the hall, Woody and Vanessa waited, smiling at her from upturned faces.

Vanessa came to the foot of the stairs to meet her. Briefly and briskly, Vanessa clasped her hand. "Super," she said. "I'm so glad you're better, and able to come downstairs. Of course, I've been wanting to pop up and visit you, but Peregrine and Woody said you didn't want to see anyone else, and I knew you were in good hands." She paused. Then she said, "You certainly look wonderfully well."

"Thank you," Angie said. She had been anxious about this encounter with Vanessa, but it was happening as easily and smoothly as Peregrine had foretold.

"Really wonderfully well," Vanessa repeated. "Peregrine, doesn't she look well?"

"She does indeed," said Peregrine, and Angie knew that it was true. She felt it, and daily the mirror confirmed it. Her eyes shone. Her cheeks were flushed. On her lips was a perpetual soft smile.

They went into the library, where a bottle of champagne stood in a silver bucket. Peregrine opened it. The cork flew up to the ceiling. They all laughed. The wine frothed into their glasses.

"To Angela," said Peregrine.

"Angela," said Vanessa.

"Angie," said Woody, with a little wink.

They raised their glasses, and drank to her. "But I can't drink to myself," she said.

"Well then," said Peregrine, "drink to the future of Foxers."

"The future of Foxers," she said, raising the glass to her lips.

"The future of Foxers," echoed Woody and Vanessa.

They all drank together How strange it was to be down here, out of her room. The room that once—it seemed so long ago and far away—she had hated. The room where, for the past two weeks, Peregrine had spent almost every moment with her.

Again and again—she never tired of it—they would recapitulate how he found her, captured her, brought her home. And saved her. Again and again—and of this *he* seemed never to tire—they would rehearse her past. The failures, the escapes, the betrayals. Each time they recited them, she understood the truth more clearly, felt it more deeply impressed upon her mind. The truth that would set her free. For the future. To fulfill her dual mission: *We shall restore my house, and you shall bear my son.*

"But what about Vanessa?" Tentatively, one evening, lying beside him, she had murmured the question. She was sipping a glass of wine—

nowadays, he gave her as much wine as she wanted.

"Vanessa wants what I want," he had said. "She loves Foxers as much as I do. And"—he spoke more slowly—"she feels as I do about my dreary brother and his sons." There was a moment's silence. Then, "Angela," he said. "I want my son to be my legal heir."

Suddenly she could see it all. Two quick divorces. Then Vanessa smiling benevolently as— bells pealing—Peregrine led Angie down the aisle. How devoted Vanessa must be to be prepared to make such a sacrifice.

"Angela," Peregrine said, "the child must seem to be Vanessa's."

She stared at him. Soothingly, he started to stroke her hair.

"Angela," he said. "I know you'll understand." So she nodded her head slowly. Then she lay still beside him. She listened.

"Vanessa has been married to me for a long time," he said. "She has never been anything but loyal to me. It isn't her fault, is it, Angela, if she is unable to have a child."

Mechanically, Angie shook her head.

"What grounds have I for discarding her?" he asked. He smiled. "Besides," he said, "she wouldn't let me. Vanessa can be very determined where her affections are involved. So you see, Angela, the only solution is for it to appear that the child is hers." Gently, he continued to stroke her hair.

"But what about me?" she said. She couldn't help it. She couldn't keep the question from her lips. "If Vanessa is the child's mother, then what shall I be?"

He cupped her face between his hands. "Why,"

he said, "the bringer of joy. Joy to him and joy to me." He kissed her, and she drowned. He drew away. He smiled down at her. "Angela," he said, "you shall be his fairy godmother."

In the walled garden, its crumbling rosy brick restored, espaliered peaches ripened for the child to pick. And Angie, from a fairy tale, hovered to protect and nurture. She would tell him stories about the cherubs on the ballroom's painted ceiling.

"His fairy godmother," she murmured.

So that became another of the matters they talked of. Angie, holding the child, by the ancient font in the church at Clave, dead Donnisthorpes blessing her from their monuments, from beneath their stones. Angie and the child, playing in the garden. "We'll make a maze," Peregrine said. "I've always wanted a maze."

But she imagined the child crying, stumbling between the baffling hedges. "I've always been afraid of mazes," she said.

Angie at Foxers. Angie, benevolent, wise, serene. And always with Peregrine. Cataloguing the books in the library. Ordering wines from a great list. Comparing swatches of material. Peregrine smiling as the blue-eyed child came running into the library, calling, "Angie! Angie, where are you?"

She never doubted that she'd have the child. It must happen; it would happen; it was her mission. But late one night, she whispered, "Peregrine, what if it's a girl?"

His roar of laughter startled her. Then, "Wonderful Angela," he said. "Wonderful Angela, how practical you are becoming! Why, Angela, if it's a girl—then we shall have to try again."

Irresistibly, she was laughing, too. "Again," she gasped. "Yes, again." Now his hands were drawing strange little cries from her. The princess would never again sleep, deep in the forest. Would never again lie, passive, frozen, in her coffin made of glass.

What a wonderful evening they were having, the four of them! Woody had prepared a positive feast for dinner. Smoked salmon, a casserole of pheasant, a chocolate mousse covered with whipped cream.

Really, Angie found the food too rich. She enjoyed the smoked salmon, but she didn't like the dark, strong taste of the pheasant. There was something musty, airless, about it, she thought, and dropped her knife and fork with a clatter on her plate.

"Is anything wrong, Angela?" Peregrine asked solicitously.

"Oh, no, nothing at all," she said hastily, taking a sip from her glass of Burgundy. It was astonishingly good.

"The last of my father's Chambertin," Peregrine had said.

They had drunk a second bottle of champagne with the smoked salmon, and they drank a third with the mousse. Angie had hardly touched the pheasant, and she found the mousse too sweet, but her glass was constantly raised to her lips.

By the time they had finished dinner, they were rivaling each other in the extravagance of their plans.

"A folly," Peregrine said. "I've always wanted a folly. A folly and a maze. But Angela won't let me have the maze. You're afraid you'll get lost in it, aren't you, Angela? So I must make do with the folly. A little temple with Doric columns. Nothing ostentatious, nothing ornate."

"We'll find one, and transport it, stone by stone," Angie promised.

"You Americans are always transporting things stone by stone," Peregrine said. And then, "Shall we find a hermit to live in the folly? That's what people did in the eighteenth century. Hire someone to live in the folly, just to look picturesque, you know. An old man with a beard."

"Yes, a long white beard," Angie agreed. "And a little lion to lie at his feet, like St. Jerome's."

"I'd rather have a horse than a hermit," Vanessa said. "A chestnut mare."

"My goodness," Woody exclaimed, "what ones you are for the wild life! What with hermits and lions and horses, I'll be too frightened to venture one step out of doors. Now what I want is a nice big refrigerator with a huge freezer compartment. I'll be able to try my hand at a lemon sorbet at last."

"How pedestrian you are, Woody." Peregrine pushed back his chair and stood up. "When we've had coffee," he said, "we'll tour the house. From the cellar to the attics."

In single file they descended the narrow stairs to the cellar. The smell of damp rose to meet them. At the bottom Peregrine switched on a dusty globe, which dimly lit only the middle of the long low-ceilinged room. Wine racks down the center stretched into darkness, and there were more racks down the sides, within arched cavernous alcoves.

"It's like a dungeon," Angie said.

"Perfect place to keep a prisoner," piped up Woody, and the silence which fell was broken by a scuffling sound from one of the alcoves.

"What was that?" Angie asked Peregrine. Woody and Vanessa were wandering ahead, between the wine racks.

"Only a rat," he said.

"A rat!" she shuddered. He rested his hand lightly on the back of her neck.

"Weren't you lucky," he said very softly, "that I didn't put you in the cellar?"

She drew in her breath. Her eyes leaped up, to meet, for a moment, an impassive blue gaze. Then he laughed. He removed his hand. "In my father's day," he said, "all these racks were filled with bottles."

Now there were a very few, single or clustered in little groups here and there. Peregrine smiled down at her. Slowly, she smiled back. "We shall fill them all again," she said.

Woody and Vanessa had turned, were coming back toward them. "Ugh," Woody said, "it isn't half chilly down here."

"We'll go back," Peregrine said, and turned to lead the way.

After the cellar, how cheerful the big kitchen looked, scattered with the homely debris of Woody's cooking. "Wouldn't you like a new stove?" Angie asked him. "A modern electric one?"

"What, be parted from my beloved Aga!" he exclaimed. "Never in a hundred years! Now, the fridge," he added, "like I said, that's quite another matter."

There were so many rooms, some half empty, some stuffed with junk, all with a neglected feeling. She found it a relief when they came to one that was familiar or inhabited.

They had paused for brandy in the library, and in the ballroom she felt suddenly lively again.

"I'd like a harp in here," she said. "Over there, by the window."

"A harp?" said Peregrine. "Angela, do you play the harp?"

"No," she said. "I just thought it would look nice."

He smiled. "Then a harp we shall have," he said.

"Pale hands I loved," sang Woody, "beside the Shalimar."

They climbed the stairs. They went from one bedroom to another. Most of them were dusty and disused. It was a shock to enter Woody's, which was tidy, chintzy, and dotted with little lamps in elaborate shades. Valentino swooned down from above his bed, and Tallulah Bankhead sulked on the opposite wall.

Peregrine and Vanessa's room had a heavy, faded grandeur. There was dark-red paper on the walls, which matched the hangings on the huge four-poster. Over the fireplace hung a portrait. Angie went over to look at it. The girl in the painting wore riding breeches and a white shirt. She leaned negligently against a five-barred gate. Fair shining hair curled just above her shoulders. Her lips pouted. Her cheeks were pink. There was a hazed dreaminess in her brown eyes. Behind the gate was a field of corn, and beyond that, green hedges. "Innocence incarnate," Peregrine murmured.

Vanessa laughed a little harshly. "Yes, I was rather sweet, wasn't I?" she said. "That was paint-

ed just before I married Peregrine," she told Angie.

They didn't go into Angie's room. When they
reached the door, she said firmly, "I know this one
already." Somehow she couldn't face the idea of
the four of them all in there together.

They climbed more stairs to the attics. Here a
wild confusion reigned. Chests and packing cases,
broken pieces of furniture, piles of ancient clothes,
were everywhere. They picked their way between
them. "I haven't been up here for ages," Vanessa
said.

In one corner stood a large rocking horse. The
paint on its round eyes and flared nostrils was
chipped and faded. Most of the tufts were missing
from its mane and tail of real horsehair. Vanessa
bestrode the horse, and started to urge it forward
and back. Each time it moved, the rocker made a
creaking sound.

Angie picked a large black velvet hat from the
floor. Great black plumes curled around its crown.
She shook it, and a cloud of dust hovered in the
air. She put the hat on her head, and went over to
look at herself in a cracked gilt mirror that was
propped against a table. Scarred by the crack in
the glass, her face stared back at her, tiny, pale,
somehow pathetic beneath the dark funereal
plumes. She shook her head. She took off the hat
and dropped it on the floor. She turned round.
Woody had wound a black lace scarf round his
head and shoulders. He half reclined against a
Victorian chaise longue which had one leg missing. He started to recite:

"How if, when I am laid into the tomb,
I wake before the time that Romeo

Come to redeem me? there's a fearful point!
Shall I not, then, be stifled in the vault,
To whose foul mouth no healthsome air
      breathes in,
And there die strangled ere my Romeo comes?"

Peregrine had picked up a sword in a battered leather scabbard. He unsheathed it. He made a thrust in the air with the blade:

> " 'Forward the Light Brigade!
> Charge for the guns!' he said:
> Into the valley of Death
> Rode the six hundred."

Woody broke in:

"Or, if I live, is it not very like,
The horrible conceit of death and night,
Together with the terror of the place,—
As in a vault, an ancient receptacle,
Where, for this many hundred years, the bones
Of all my buried ancestors are pack'd:
Where bloody Tybalt, yet but green in earth,
Lies festering in his shroud. . . ."

"Christ, Woody, do shut up!" Peregrine shouted. He made another thrust in the air with his sword. He declaimed:

> "Storm'd at with shot and shell,
> Boldly they rode and well,
> Into the jaws of Death,
> Into the mouth of Hell. . . ."

The rocking horse creaked as, on and on, oblivious, Vanessa rode.

That night, for the first time, Angie's door was not locked. She lay waiting for Peregrine. And just as the first light filtered in through the curtains, as the first bird chirruped, at last he came, opening the door softly, moving silently toward the bed. Sighing with joy, she opened her arms.

She'd never been so happy, never felt so well. There was so much to plan, so much to do.

It was a week after she first came downstairs that she telephoned Dr. Blaumann. In spite of all those things he'd said about him, it was Peregrine who suggested it.

"Won't that doctor of yours be worrying about you?" he asked.

"Why, yes," she said. "I suppose he may be."

It was strange to hear Dr. Blaumann's voice again. "Angela," he said warmly, when the receptionist had put her through, "how are you?"

"I'm fine," she said. "Just fine."

"I'm very glad to hear that," he said.

She told him that she had left the cottage. "I found it too much, being on my own."

"Yes," he said, and then, "I thought you might."

She told him that she was staying with friends, that she was helping to restore an old house. "Admirable," he said. "Admirable, Angela. A worthwhile purpose. A communal project. I can't think of anything more appropriate, more constructive." There was a pause. "And how," he asked, "is your book coming along?"

"Oh," she said. "I've given that up. I decided I

didn't really enjoy doing it. I'm finding what I'm doing now much more rewarding."

"And who are these people you are staying with?"

"Oh," she said, "a married couple. They've been so kind to me."

"A family situation," he said. "Yes, that is excellent also. Angela, you have my best wishes. If at any time you feel you need to see me, of course you have only to get in touch. Or perhaps you would like to come and have a little talk in the near future? Would you like to make an appointment?"

"Oh, no," she said. "Thank you very much, but I don't think so. I really don't feel like coming up to London at the moment."

Why should she want to go to London, or to see Dr. Blaumann, when she had everything she wanted here? The plans for the future of Foxers. And Peregrine. Every night and every day.

The days went so quickly. Three weeks had passed since she had telephoned Dr. Blaumann. It was afternoon, and she was sitting in the library. She was especially happy today, so happy that she found it difficult to concentrate on the letter she was writing to the storage company in London, asking them to send down her books and her father's desk and chair. Peregrine had bought two magnificent new bookcases for the library at an auction. She wanted to have the desk and chair in her own room.

She finished the letter. As she signed her name, she heard a car draw up on the gravel, and wondered idly who it could be. The Donnisthorpes never seemed to have callers. "We've been hermits for too long, I'm afraid," Peregrine had said. But she was glad. She didn't want to see anyone else.

There were voices in the hall. Then Peregrine opened the library door. "I've got a surprise for you," he said. "A visitor." And there she was. Jessica. She was wearing a turquoise dress; a matching scarf was tied round her neat little head.

"Darling Angie," she exclaimed as Angie ran forward to meet her. Jessica's cheek was smooth against Angie's lips. Jessica's familiar Diorissima enveloped her.

Peregrine was still standing in the doorway, smiling. "I'll leave you two alone," he said. "I'm sure you must have a lot to talk about." He went out, closing the door behind him.

"Jessica," Angie said. "Oh, Jessica!"

"Darling, you're looking too wonderful," Jessica said.

"Yes, I feel wonderful." Angie nodded. "Oh, Jessica, I've never been so happy." Impulsively again, she pressed her lips to Jessica's cheek. And then she said, "But what are you doing here? How did you know?"

"That you were here? I've got a confession to make to you." Jessica wandered over to the fireplace, traced a circle, with her finger, on the face of the carriage clock that stood on the mantelpiece. She turned to face Angie, resting one slim foot, in a high-heeled sandal, on the edge of the grate.

"How brown you are," Angie said.

"Yes, I've been abroad."

"Cecily told me," Angie said. They were suddenly stilled. A silence fell between them. Angie broke it. "You said you had a confession to make?"

"Well, yes." Jessica opened her handbag, and took out a packet of Gauloise. She offered them to Angie, and then took one herself, lighting both cigarettes with a little gold lighter that had been, Angie remembered, Richard's bridesmaid's present to her.

"I told the Donnisthorpes about you," Jessica said. "I was worried about your being alone in that cottage, and I asked them to keep an eye on you. It seems," she smiled, "that my scheme succeeded admirably." Her eyes glittered. There was a mischievous expression on her face. "Better than I could ever have imagined," she said. And then, "Ah, Angie, you still have your blush, I see." She blew a perfect smoke ring. It drifted in the air between them for a moment, and then dissolved.

"I rather fancy myself in the role of pimp," Jessica said, and giggled.

"Oh, Jessica," Angie said, "you're as dreadful as ever."

"Mmm. I rather thought you'd fall for Peregrine," Jessica said. "I know you." Some memory—what was it? Kirsty on the stairs: *I know you.* Angie shivered, feeling a sudden chill.

"So everything," Jessica said, "has worked out for the best. All for the best in the best of all possible worlds, as they say. You're really happy?"

"Oh, yes, so happy," Angie said. And then, "I understand everything now. I've made a whole new beginning."

"The slate wiped clean. A fresh start. It's very

seldom one can do that. Lucky Angie!" Jessica dropped her cigarette stub into the empty grate. "Angie," she said, "I've come to ask you something. I want you to help me."

"Oh, Jessica," Angie said. She felt a rush of affection. Dear Jessica! After all, in a way, wasn't Jessica responsible for her present happiness. "I'll do anything I can," she said. "Anything."

"I want to go to him," Jessica said.

"To him?"

"I want to go to Richard."

"To Richard?" She was stunned. She vibrated with the shock of it. His name quivered in the air between them.

"Yes. I have to go to him. To be with him always. I've seen him. But it isn't enough. I, too, Angie—I have to start again."

"You love him," Angie stated. The idea was extraordinary. And yet, now, suddenly, she felt she'd always known it. As if a picture which she'd passed a hundred times without noticing it had suddenly sprung to life before her eyes.

"Always," Jessica said. "Since we were children." She turned again to face the clock. "Forbidden games. That wild excitement. There was a place in the woods." Her voice faltered. She broke off.

"And he loves you," Angie said.

"Oh, yes. Dear Richard." There was some irony in Jessica's tone now. "But, of course, it never could have worked in those days. Neither of us was really equipped for holy poverty, love in a cottage. Especially not Richard."

"So when he married me . . ." She left the sentence unfinished.

"Yes, darling, I'm afraid so." Again Jessica's finger traced the circle of the clock face. Then she turned round. "Do you remember a letter?" she said.

"A letter?" Angie's mind was blank.

"A letter you got in Cleveland. He put it in the wrong envelope. I got the letter he wrote to you."

She remembered now. *My fierce wild girl . . . I deserve whatever treatment you mete out to me.* The forgotten phrases rose from the past. Another piece of a jigsaw was laid precisely in its place.

"And after we were married, you carried on?"

"Yes. Though, at one time, I did try not to. I married Simon. But Simon was really just a shadow of Richard, wasn't he? And a shadow wasn't enough."

"I see." She couldn't help feeling a sense of betrayal. Not betrayal by Richard, though. Betrayal by Jessica.

"And . . . Kirsty?" she asked.

Jessica's face closed. "Yes, that was his one lapse. I didn't mind about you. You were something different. And, with you, it never worked, did it?"

"No," Angie said. "It never worked."

"But she . . . oh, how I hated that woman, Angie. I knew it would be only a matter of time till he came back to me. But how I loathed her. I wanted her to die. I was glad when he killed her."

"Yes," Angie said. "And then?"

"He turned to me, of course. He turned to me. And I arranged everything." She laughed triumphantly. "I've always been a good organizer."

Her voice softened. "I remember when I went to see you in the hospital. I was right in the thick of it then. I was out of my mind with worry. That's why I was so horrid to you. I was desperate. I'm sorry, Angie."

"Oh, that's all right," she heard herself say politely.

Jessica lit another cigarette. She shook her head dismissively. "Anyway, as we were saying—weren't we?—it's all for the best. Isn't it, Angie?" And suddenly there were tears in Jessica's eyes. She brushed at them angrily with her hand.

Angie realized she'd never seen Jessica cry. Suddenly, sympathy overwhelmed her. "Oh, Jessica," she said. "Please don't cry." She took a step toward her. She placed a hand on her arm.

"Darling Angie," Jessica said, still brushing at her eyes, "you're so sweet."

And after all, Angie thought, wasn't it for the best? Her happiness flooded back, making her wise, making her strong, making her able to accept everything. Jessica's betrayal—wasn't it old history, to be forgiven even if never quite forgotten?

"Jessica," she said, "I want to help you. Just tell me how I can?"

The tears were gone from Jessica's eyes now. She gave a little shrug of her shoulders. "I'm sorry," she said. "It's the usual thing. I need money, Angie. Money to go away with. Money for us to live on, abroad, in hiding."

"Money?" Angie said. She smiled. "That's easy." Here she was again. The bringer of joy. The fairy godmother.

Jessica had turned toward the mantelpiece

again. "I'll just go upstairs and get my check-book," Angie said.

Upstairs in her room, she took the checkbook out of her bag. She sat down on the bed. What figure should she make the check out for? she wondered. She wanted it to contain the number three. Three was the number in the fairy tales: the third son, the third dress—the one in which the princess finally dazzled the prince. And three, she thought, was *their* number, too. Hers and Richard's and Jessica's.

Thirty thousand pounds was the sum she wrote. She folded the check in half, and took it down-stairs. In the library, Jessica still stood by the man-telpiece.

"Here you are," she said, and handed Jessica the folded check. Suddenly she was aware of some-thing she had long forgotten—Jessica's pouncing, catlike look. She almost snatched the check from Angie's hand. She opened it. Then, "Darling Angie," she said.

Jessica moved toward the window. "Angie," she said, "what are you doing about a divorce? Not that it worries me at all. Richard and I can't get married. What would be the point, anyway? But I can't help wondering if you've made a will."

"A will?" Angie said. "No, I haven't done that. The lawyers are always writing about it. They want to set up some kind of foundation. But I just haven't got around to it. Why?"

Jessica said, "I was just thinking that if any-thing happened to you, then everything would go to Richard. Though of course he wouldn't be able to claim it. But don't you think you should sort that out?"

"Why, yes," Angie said. "I hadn't thought about

it. I must do something soon. You're quite right."

Jessica picked up her handbag, which she had dropped on the sofa. She was carefully putting the check away in a pocket inside it. Then she closed the bag with a snap, and came toward Angie. "I must go now," she said.

"Oh, can't you stay?" Angie said. "Since you know Peregrine. And Vanessa. You could stay for dinner. You could stay the night. We could talk some more."

"No," Jessica said. "No, darling Angie. I must go. I've got so many things to do." There was a moment of silence.

"Tell Richard," Angie said, "that I wish him well. I wish you both well."

"Steady, darling," Jessica said. She was laughing; she was crying again. "Don't become *too* saintly," she said. "It's unnerving for the rest of us. Good-bye, Angie." Jessica's lips were on Angie's cheek. The Diorissima was in Angie's nostrils. Then Jessica was hurrying to the door, raising her left hand in salute as she opened it, but not looking back.

Angie heard the car start up on the gravel. She sighed. She sat down on the sofa. A sudden melancholy and unease possessed her. Then she heard the door open. It was Peregrine. He came in, closing the door behind him, and sat down beside her on the sofa. He took her hand.

"Well?" he said.

"Well!" she said. "Now I know who told you so much about me."

He laughed. "I know everything about you, Angela," he said. He raised her hand to his lips, and kissed it.

She could feel the brilliance of her smile as she said to him, "Not *quite* everything." And then, as he raised his eyebrows, "Peregrine, I think I'm pregnant."

FOUR

It was true. First, Woody took a specimen to a London pregnancy-testing service. The result was positive, and a week later, the doctor confirmed it.

The doctor was an old friend of Peregrine's. There was something a little shabby, a little seedy, about him, she thought. Perhaps she got that impression from his ancient gingery tweeds, from the smelly pipe he puffed at all the time. Anyway, he was a good doctor. Peregrine assured her of that: "Would I trust you, would I trust our child, to anyone who wasn't?" The doctor was going to come to see her every month, and would come to stay in the house shortly before the child was due. "We shall take very good care of you," Peregrine promised.

And, of course, they were doing that already: Vanessa, constantly inquiring about her health; Woody, fussing around her, making special dishes to tempt her appetite—she felt sick in the mornings, but the doctor had told her that that would soon pass. And Peregrine was doing all the things she'd dreamed of: ordering wine with her, looking at catalogues, always kind and solicitous.

Too solicitous, in one way, she couldn't help feeling. On the night after the doctor's visit, he had come to her room. She had held out her arms to him, as she always did, but this time he shook his head, sitting down on the side of the bed, and taking her hand.

"I spoke to the doctor," he said, "and really it isn't very good for you." He searched for a phrase, settled on "that kind of thing." Then, "I must restrain myself," he said, and, with the smile that always made her melt, "difficult though that is going to be."

She'd always heard that it was quite all right, for the first few months anyway. But if the doctor had said not, then she supposed that that must be wrong. Now Peregrine was saying, "I feel superstitious about it, too. I couldn't bear to do anything that might damage the child, or you." He kissed her forehead; he kissed her hands; he went away. Now he never came to her room at night.

But the days were so wonderful. A landscape gardener came down from London, and they walked the garden with him, making plans. Leaves rustled beneath their feet. The smell of fall was in the air.

The evenings were getting colder. Angie spoke wistfully of central heating. "Rather stuffy, I always think," Vanessa said. Anyway, as Peregrine pointed out, installing it right away, when there were so many other things to do, would really cause too much of an upheaval.

"Next year," he promised. "In the summer. We'll have it put in before the cold weather."

Ever since Jessica's visit, Angie had been brooding on the subject of her will. At last she spoke to Peregrine about it.

"A will, Angela?" he said. "Now you mustn't start becoming morbid." He smiled. "People don't die in childbirth these days. And certainly not beautiful healthy girls like you."

"It's not that," she said. "It was something Jessica said: that if anything happened to me, all the money would go to Richard. Of course, he couldn't claim it, but the whole situation's so untidy. And, besides, the lawyers keep writing to me about it." She got up from the sofa, and came over to stand next to the red armchair in which he always sat. "Peregrine," she said, "I'm going to leave everything to you."

"To me, Angela?" he said. "No I can't allow you to do that. And besides, in the course of nature, you will survive me by many years."

"To you and your heirs," she said firmly. She laughed. "Did you think I was going to leave our child unprovided for?"

She wrote to Mr. Hawthorne, her father's lawyer in Cleveland, telling him about her intentions, and received an obviously anxious letter back. "I really feel that I must see you," he wrote, "before you take such a wholly unexpected decision."

When she told Peregrine, he said, "Of course, he's perfectly right. He would be a most unsatisfactory lawyer if he didn't look after your interests. Get him to come over from America. Ask him down here for a day."

"Why, Angie," he said as he got out of the car, "how well you're looking. It's been so many years, and so many things have happened." She could see that he was thinking about Richard and the case. "But you've changed so little," he went on. "You're put on a touch of weight, perhaps, but it certainly suits you. You were always such a frail little girl."

His hair was almost white. How strange it was to see him here at Foxers, dry and neat in his dark conservative business suit.

How proud she was of Peregrine! She'd never seen him more charming than he was that day. It was astonishing to see how quickly Mr. Hawthorne thawed.

Woody didn't have lunch with them. He waited at table. He had abandoned his T-shirt and jeans for dark trousers and a waiter's white tunic which he had bought in Bury on the previous day. As he filled Mr. Hawthorne's glass for the third time, he gave Angie one of his winks. She had to turn aside hastily in order not to burst out laughing.

"A real British aristocrat, Sir Peregrine," Mr. Hawthorne said as he and Angie settled down in the library after lunch. "A very fine type of man, I've always heard, and now I can believe it."

She told him how kind the Donnisthorpes had been to her. "You know how ill I've been at times?" He nodded sympathetically. "Well, that's all over now," she said.

"But can you be sure of that?" he asked gently.

"Yes," she said. "Because, at last, I've found a real home."

They sorted out a lot of things that afternoon, among them the quietest and quickest way of putting her divorce through. When it came to the will, he queried her provision that the money she left to Peregrine should go to his heirs.

"Who will *they* be?" he asked.

"Vanessa," she told him, "is going to have a child."

"Is she now?" he said, surprised. "Why, I never would have guessed that."

"It's still early," Angie said. "She's not expecting it till next summer."

"Don't you think, Angie," he asked her, "that you may marry again some day, and have children of your own?"

She shook her head decisively. "I've had enough of marriage," she told him.

"Well, I suppose I can understand that, in the circumstances," he said, "but perhaps you'll change your ideas some day, if you meet the right person. Some nice neighbor of Sir Peregrine's, perhaps?" He smiled. "Anyhow," he said, "if that eventuality arises, you can always make another will."

As he climbed, rather stiffly, into the chauffeur-driven hired car, she felt a pang, as if she were severing her last link with the past. He was probably the last person she would ever see who had known her father. She waved rather desperately after the departing car. Peregrine was beside her. He took her arm, and led her into the house.

As she lay in bed that night, she reflected on how well organized she was becoming. Everything was falling into place. Everything was wonderful. Except one thing. How she longed for Peregrine! Tonight, as on every night since the doctor's visit, she hungered, thirsted, yearned for him in the darkness. Had she the strength to bear it? Suddenly, she didn't think so. Wasn't there some way, she wondered, that she could change his mind?

It was at lunch the next day that she learned that Woody and Vanessa were going shopping in Bury that afternoon. After lunch, as usual, she went up to her room for the rest which they now encouraged her to take each day. But she didn't lie down. She watched from a window in the corridor till she saw them get into the car and drive away. Then she went into her room.

She stood in front of the mirror. She made up her face. She brushed her hair. She scented herself with Bellodgia. She took off her clothes. From the bottom drawer of the bow-fronted chest she fetched the skirt torn from waist to hem, the embroidered blouse ripped from neck to waist. She put them on her naked body, leaving the blouse hanging open, loosely knotting the torn waistband of the skirt.

As she went along the corridor, she was conscious of the floorboards beneath her bare feet. As she descended the staircase, she imagined slow music. Her hand trailed on the banister.

He was asleep in the library, in the red armchair, as she had known he would be. She approached him on tiptoe. She bent over him. She pressed her mouth against his, and he opened his eyes.

She stepped back. His glance took her in from head to toe. Her heart was pounding. Then he closed his eyes.

She stepped forward again. She kissed, one after the other, his closed lids. She kissed them; she ran her tongue over them, and kissed them again. She nibbled gently along his eyebrows, along the line of his hair, with little kisses.

She returned to his lips. She slid her tongue between them, and ran it along his teeth. They parted, and she let her tongue rest on his, then circled it over the roof of his mouth. But her obsession was with pressing her lips against his, drinking from them as if parched, sucking at them as if she would never be able to taste enough of them.

How could she bear to leave his mouth? But eventually her lips slid down his neck, grazing in the hollow of his throat as she undid the buttons of his shirt. Standing bowed over him, she dragged her nipples, which swelled like berries, across his chest. The edges of her torn blouse brushed loosely across his ribs. She rested her head on his heart, listening to its calm, steady beat as she circled his nipples with her tongue. Then she lifted each of his hands in turn, and planted a deep kiss in the palm.

And now she swung herself up so that she was sitting on his knees, her feet in the chair, on either side of his thighs. Neatly, delicately, her fingers undid his buttons. She took his penis in her hand, and she rubbed its tip against her pale pubic hairs. Then she slid it into her in one smooth movement. And then she wriggled, and turned, and moaned, and laughed, and, at last, for one moment, rested her head against his heart again. It was beating faster now.

Slowly she drew away from him. Then she was on her knees, parting his thighs with her hands, then pressing them, with her elbows, against her sides as she took his penis into her mouth, and, in one long shudder, he came. She swallowed his seed like a sacrament.

Last of all, she kissed his mouth once more, deeply, wanting to drown him in the taste of himself mingled with the taste of her. Then she stood up. She turned. Vanessa was standing in the doorway.

"I came back to fetch my checkbook," Vanessa

said in a loud high voice. She was looking past Angie, at Peregrine, who opened his eyes, who leaped to his feet as Angie, head held high, went past Vanessa into the hall. As she started to climb the stairs, she heard Vanessa say, "*That* was never part of the bargain."

She lay down on her bed. Yes, it had been unfortunate, but after all, hadn't Vanessa consented to so much more than that? Everything would be all right by tomorrow, she decided. Meanwhile, today, it would probably be tactful to keep out of sight. She closed her eyes. She smiled. *She didn't care.* In a little while she fell asleep.

She tiptoed to the gallery at about seven that evening, when she knew Woody would be bustling about, carrying drinks to the library, laying the dining-room table. When he came into the hall, she called to him softly. He looked up, put the tray he was carrying on the hall table, and came hurrying up the stairs. "And what have *you* been up to?" he said quite grimly. And then, "But we haven't time to go into that now."

"Could you bring me a tray upstairs, do you think?" she asked him. "I'm feeling a bit tired tonight," she added, trying not to show the strange triumph that filled her.

But she didn't succeed. "Goodness gracious, how pleased with herself she's feeling," Woody said tartly. "And I'm sure I can't imagine why."

She went back to her room, and brushed her hair, and looked at herself in the long mirror. She was lying on her bed, smiling at the ceiling, when Woody came up with cold chicken and salad. "Mmm," she said dreamily. "It looks delicious."

"More than you deserve," he said. "It ought to be bread and water for *you* tonight." And when she giggled, he snapped, "No, you're a very silly girl," and almost flounced from the room. What was the matter with *him*? she wondered.

When she had eaten her supper, she picked up *Grimm's Fairy Tales*, and read the story of Cinderella.

. . . When she stood up, the prince recognized the beautiful maiden who had danced with him, and cried, 'This is the true bride!'

The stepmother and the two sisters turned pale with rage, but he took Cinderella upon his horse, and rode away with her.

As they passed by the hazel-tree, the two white pigeons cried,

> Turn and look, turn and look,
>   No blood is in the shoe.
> The shoe is not too small for her.
> The true bride rides with you.

And the two came flying down and perched on Cinderella's shoulders, one on the right, the other on the left, and stayed there till they reached the palace.

She woke to hear someone moving in her room. She smiled. She stretched. "Peregrine," she murmured.

"No, *not* Peregrine, Angie. What would he be doing here at this hour of night, away from the conjugal couch?" Woody sat down on the bed. Moonlight was flooding in through the windows. Woody's eyes gleamed brightly.

"I've made up my mind," he said. "You've got to go."

"To *go*?" she echoed.

"Yes, and tonight. Right away. While I've got the nerve. Woody has screwed his courage to the sticking point, as the Bard put it—rather indelicately, if I may say so."

"Woody, what *are* you talking about?" she said.

"Angie, I've decided to help you."

How serious he sounded. She didn't know how to respond. "That's sweet of you," she said.

"Oh, ever so sweet of me, I'm sure. You sound as if I'd asked you to a garden party. Angie, I'm trying to save your life."

"To save my life?" she repeated.

"Yes, and I'll have you know, I'm risking my own in the process. Greater love hath no man, as they say."

"But what can you mean?" she said.

"Haven't you ever wondered 'what the future holds,' as the crystal-gazers put it? No, seriously, Angie, haven't you speculated about where all this is leading? I mean, when the blessèd babe is born, and the welcoming carols have been sung, et cetera, et cetera. No, I can see from your face that you haven't. You really are a dozy one, aren't you?"

She shook her head blankly.

He went on. "If it's a girl, dear, well, that may be all right. Because you know, for the inheritance, it's got to be a boy. So back to the drawing board. Charming, I'm sure, if you like that sort of thing, and it seems, dear, that you do, these days. But if it's the longed-for son and heir, first time lucky—well, lucky for some—what role precisely do you see yourself playing, may I ask?"

"Why, things will go on just as they do now,"

Angie said. "People will think the baby's Vanessa's. But I'll be able to spend a lot of time with it. And we'll go on restoring the house. . . ."

"And Peregrine will creep into your bed from time to time, no doubt?"

She was silent.

"My dear," he said, "you *are* living in a fool's paradise, and no mistake. Hasn't it occurred to you what a danger you'll be to them?"

"A danger?"

"Able to spill the beans at any minute. You're not renowned for your stability, now, are you? Do you really think they'd take the risk of keeping you around? And do you really imagine that Vanessa appreciates your presence?"

"Peregrine wants me here," she said proudly.

"Frankly, ducky, I don't think Peregrine gives a damn. And don't smile in that silly way. Just because he gave in gracefully to your importunities today. Peregrine won't allow anyone to deflect him from his course."

"What course, Woody?"

"The course he's been following all along. Do you really think that the way he's treated you shows *concern* for you?"

"Oh, yes," she said. "Why, of course it does. Woody, he's given me everything. He saved me from my madness."

"Angie, you must be madder than you've ever been before if you believe that. When he deliberately set out to *drive* you mad."

"Woody, what are you talking about? Peregrine taught me to face the truth. About myself. About my hallucinations."

"What hallucinations, Angie?" Woody's eyes gleamed again in the moonlight.

"Why, at the cottage," she said. "All those terrible things I thought I saw and heard."

"The things you saw and heard, Angie—you saw and heard them all."

What could he mean? She stared at him. She took a cigarette from the packet on the bedside table, and lit it, though she'd promised Peregrine she'd try to stop smoking because of the baby.

"Goodness, Angie, honestly, I've never been so busy in my life. The stone head the first day, and those drops in your drink, to knock you out. We were watching you all the time from the cottage next door, when you thought we were away. Letting you simmer. And then I put those words in your story, and typed a fresh sheet when you were wandering around the village, pissed out of your mind. And then, do you remember the morning when you came up to the cottage next door? Vanessa saw you from the window upstairs, and called, and I crouched down under the window but I thought you might be able to see me, so I drew the curtains. That was a moment of suspense, all right! and then the last night. That laugh of mine was really quite an achievement. I got it from the witch in Disney's *Snow White*, as a matter of fact. I used to practice it here, and we'd all go into fits. And Vanessa, scratching at your window with a long broom, after she'd put that bag of old clothes with the tomato ketchup all over it in the hall. When Peregrine got you into the car, how we did bustle round! Lugging the bag over the fence next door, and then nipping into the other car, and racing back here to welcome you. Yes, that was a night, that was, and all!"

"Stop," she said. "I don't believe you. I don't believe a word of it."

"You'd better, Angie. You'd better use that head of yours, for once. If you want to save your life. Because it's your life that's at stake. They're going to kill you, Angie. Sooner or later, they're going to kill you. Once they've got the son and heir. Do you think, with your record, people would find it difficult to believe you were a suicide?"

"But Woody," she said, "if all this were true, surely you were involved in it, too."

"Well," he said, "it all seemed like a game, to begin with. I was always one for a nice touch of drama, you know. It was like being in a play, really, working it all out, and learning one's part. And then, when you came here, well, I did think he went a bit too far. But it wasn't long before there you were like a cat that had swallowed the cream. And I didn't let myself see the truth. I didn't let myself realize they were actually going to kill you. Really I didn't. Till today, that is. You see, I heard them talking in the library this afternoon, when he was trying to quiet her down. Reminding her. He spelled it out in black and white."

A band of ice was closing around her heart. "What shall I do?" she said. "Woody, I don't know what to do."

"There's petrol in your car," he said. "I've parked it down at the bottom of the drive. You must go back to London."

"Woody, I can't," she said.

"Angie, you must."

There was a moment's silence. "Woody," she said, "will you come with me?"

He shook his head. "Oh, no, Angie," he said. "It's too late for me. Too late to teach a poor old bitch like me new tricks. I belong here at Foxers. I'm one of the fixtures, you could say. And really, as you know, I owe everything to Peregrine. Loyal to the school, that's me. Just an old-fashioned girl. Guide's honor, you know. Except this once. And, Angie, that's something *you've* got to do for *me*. You must never tell anybody a word about any of this. You must never tell anybody that I helped you. More than my place is worth," he added, and then, in a different tone, "Peregrine would kill *me* if he found out. Really, he would. I know it. Disloyalty—that's one thing he could never forgive."

"I can't bear it. Any of it," she said.

"You've just got to. Angie, you've got to make it on your own from now on. First, I'd say, go to some nice doctor. Plenty of doctors who'll help a girl in trouble. Especially with *your* money," he added, with a touch of astringency. "You find some nice posh clinic, and get yourself fixed up. And then go away, go back to America, make a fresh start. And keep away from old green-eyes. That Jessica. You can be sure she's in it, up to the hilt. Expecting her ten percent—or more, if I judge that one rightly—when the will goes through."

"The will," she said. "Oh, yes, of course. The will."

She dressed and, taking only her handbag, tiptoed after Woody, along the corridor, holding her sandals in her hand. She paused at the top of the staircase, under the portrait of Peregrine's mother, glancing along the gallery to the dim shape of the grand piano. And then she followed him down the stairs, in the darkness and silence, to the hall. He slid back the bolt on the front door, and turned the great handle, and the cold night air came in to meet them. He kissed her cheek. "Goodbye, Angie," he had whispered. "*Silence à la mort*. You're free."

The door closed softly behind her. The gravel was white in the moonlight. The dark trees beckoned her toward the drive. How loudly the gravel crunched under her sandals, even though she was walking on tiptoe. She was conscious of the blank windows of the house behind her, but she did not look back. *When Orpheus had rescued Eurydice from the underworld, he had broken his promise, and had looked back, and on the very threshold of life she had been lost to him.*

Now at last she was in the shelter of the trees. It was very dark. Leaves rustled under her feet. There were little movements in the undergrowth. Suddenly she wanted to run, but running seemed an invitation to someone—or something—to follow. So she kept on walking, in the very center of the drive. The sudden scream of some small animal, dying or trapped, froze her, but after a moment she went on. How long the drive was! But at last the white five-barred gate glinted ahead of her in the moonlight.

The car was parked on the grass verge outside. She went through the gate, and closed it behind her. She took the keys to the car, which Woody had given her, from her bag, and opened the car door and got inside. She felt like just sitting there, behind the steering wheel. But she knew she must get moving, must get away. There would be plenty of time—so much time—to rest, to think, later. She started the car. She drove along by the wall, and turned, left, into the lane.

Past the cottage with the gnomes in the garden,

over the bridge, past the church where she'd never been to look at the misericord seats—*Oh, Jessica!* And she reached the end of the little tunnel of lane, and turned left, onto the road that led to London.

"You're free." She kept repeating those words of Woody's, over and over again in her mind. Why didn't they mean anything to her?

How slowly she was driving! But it was nearly dawn, and London was getting nearer all the time.

"You're free."

She was at the edge of Epping Forest. She drew to the side of the road. In the silence when she switched off the engine, she could hear the birds beginning to sing. *"You're free."* The sky was growing pale. The moon was fading into it. The peacock would be waking in the garden at Foxers. The dead twigs of the Weeping Wellingtonia—*"I rather like it dead"*—would be silhouetted against the dark branches of the trees beyond the lawn.

When she got to London, where would she go? To a hotel? Brown's? Or somewhere quieter? Perhaps one of those terrible private places, with pillars, in the Cromwell Road? Or some great impersonal palace where she would pass quite unnoticed? The one at Marble Arch, where no one but tourists ever stayed, piling into their coaches after a night or two, heading for Stratford-upon-Avon. There she could take refuge in some blank, clean little "room with bath," order things from room service, and just lie on the bed until she had sorted everything out. *You're free.*

Whom would she see? Dr. Blaumann? But what

would he be able to do for her? After all, she couldn't tell him anything that had happened.

Suddenly she thought of Joe. He must have been back from the States for ages now. Would he still be in the studio off the Fulham Road? What would he say if she turned up there? He might have some girl with him. Should she risk that? Dear Joe. He had been so sweet. But somehow, just at the moment, she couldn't remember his face. Only that old brown velour sweater that had made him remind her of a mole.

> The lovely lady, Christabel,
> Whom her father loves so well,
> What makes her in the wood so late,
> A furlong from the castle gate?

How loud the birds were singing now. And there was a brilliance in the sky. She started the engine.

As she swept onto the gravel, the little stones rattling against the side of the car, she saw Woody's face at the window, absolutely incredulous. She wanted to laugh. Then all three of them were on the steps. She saw that Woody's eyes were full of tears. But Vanessa's face looked as if it had been carved out of ice, frozen, rigid, deadly pale.

Angie got out of the car. Her eyes were fixed on Peregrine. And he sprang toward her, his arms extended. How his blue gaze dazzled her! "I knew you would," he said. "I knew that you'd come home." She buckled at the knees, and he picked her up in his arms, and, once more, carried her, as if she were a child—yes, she felt like a child again —her head against his chest, her knees dangling over his arm. Past Woody and Vanessa. Into the hall, and then into the library, where he sat down in the red chair, still holding her in his arms.

It was a very cold winter that year. Soon after dinner, every night, Woody went upstairs to light the fire in her bedroom, and draw the curtains, and put a hot-water bottle in her bed. She became tired easily nowadays, and usually she was in bed by half after nine. "Good night," Vanessa would say, politely but perfunctorily, glancing up from her slow perusal of *The Times*. "Night-night," Woody would carol. And Peregrine would rise from the red chair, and come up the stairs with her, his hand beneath her elbow. They would go along the corridor together, and when they reached her door, he would open it and switch on the light for her. He would kiss her forehead, and she would go inside. "Good night, Angela," he would say, and then he would shut the door, and she would hear him turn the key in the lock. To keep her safe. How lovely it was, lying curled in bed with the firelight flickering on the walls.

How busy things were in the daytime! There were men clearing the garden; there were painters in the house. Three Italian craftsmen were working on the ballroom ceiling. An older man, gray-haired and thickset, and two dark young boys. She dredged up Italian phrases she had heard her father use, and they would smile and laugh and say, "*Si, Signorina.*" Sometimes Peregrine would pour them glasses of Chianti, and Woody would bring them a great dish piled high with pasta. It was such fun, though she realized that soon, when her pregnancy became apparent, she'd have to stay upstairs in her room whenever people were about. Vanessa was already starting to wear loose smocks over her trousers.

Of course, Angie hoped that the child would be a girl, because then they'd have to try again. Peregrine would come to her bed for the long nights, and she would wake in his arms to hear the peacock screeching on the lawn. But even if it was a boy, there would be so many things to do. She would be godmother in the church at Clave. *The dead Donnisthorpes would bless her from their monuments, from beneath their stones.* And Peregrine— well, she felt sure that even if it were a boy, she'd find some way to make him want her. After all, she had done so once before. . . .

Her greatest pleasure was to sit with him, alone, in the library. Just watching him. He would look up from his accounts or his book, and give her his beautiful, sometimes oddly weary smile. He was so wonderful to her. He had made her give up smoking completely. He made sure she took her milk and orange juice, and he only allowed her to drink three glasses of wine a day: one from the split of champagne he would open for the two of them every morning at eleven, one with lunch, and one with dinner.

When Peregrine was out, or busy, she often sat in the conservatory, reading fairy stories. And sometimes she and Woody played silly games like snap or checkers. He was always nice to her, but they didn't chat in the way they used to. There seemed to be a gap, almost a coldness, between them.

Of course she knew that that was due to what she thought of as "the problem." The problem was the only thing that really worried her: the fact that Woody had told her all those lies. She'd thought about it a lot, and she had finally decided that Woody had been jealous, that he hadn't been able to bear the importance of the part she played at Foxers. Poor Woody! And now he was feeling guilty, and that was why he seemed so remote from her.

She often thought that she ought to bring it all out into the open. For Woody's sake—everything would be so much easier and more natural afterward. But there was another reason, too. A more important one.

She couldn't bear to feel that she had a secret from Peregrine. It seemed like a betrayal of his trust. In her heart she knew that she would, that she must, tell him. She wanted to a little more each day. After she told him, then, at last, she would be truly free. She would be home. She would be safe. She would be his forever.

Keep Up With The BESTSELLERS!